WHEN PENGUINS FLY

An Ascension Enhancement Project

Andrew Patrick Timothy Michael Craig

Author's Tranquility Press
ATLANTA, GEORGIA

Andrew Patrick Timothy Michael Craig/Author's Tranquility Press
3900 N Commerce Dr. Suite 300 #1255
Atlanta, GA 30344, USA
www.authorstranquilitypress.com

Ordering Information:
Quantity sales. Special discounts are available on quantity purchases by corporations, associations, and others. For details, contact the "Special Sales Department" at the address above.

When Penguins Fly: An Ascension Enhancement Project Andrew Patrick Timothy Michael Craig
Library of Congress Control Number: 2024923806
Hardback: 978-1-964810-59-1
Paperback: 978-1-964810-41-6
eBook: 978-1-964810-42-3

CONTENTS

NOTICE: This book presents an entertaining story that may in some way assist those intending to move to the Fifth Dimension of Consciousness (the 5DC). To move to the 5DC requires greater integrity and ethics than is currently evident in the dominant level of consciousness upon planet Earth. For instance, there are no victims in the 5DC because the Law of Attraction is universally operative in the 5DC and as such anything and everything that happens to a being in the 5DC is because the being attracted it to them. Accordingly, there is always at least a powerful personal teaching in any seemingly unpleasant reactions. This book may be quite confrontational for those with lesser integrity and ethics than that. It is strongly recommended that you do not read this book if you do not accept complete and sole responsibility for any reactions you may have to anything you read within this book. Additionally, it is strongly recommended that you do not read this book if your physical, mental, and emotional bodies are not sound.

Andrew Patrick Timothy Michael Craig

WELCOME

Beautiful, blessed, and beloved one. Welcome to this ascension initiating conversation for your Mother Earth and her species of Human Beings of which you are a part. The mere act of you acquiring this book and opening it to this page and commencing reading it is positively influencing our ascension quest even if you relate to the story as only science fiction. The science of consciousness is still poorly developed and so science and spirit seem at opposite ends of the spectrum of reality so to speak. But consciousness is where they will overlap. So, you are already playing a part in this event and the longer and deeper you move into the conversation the greater that part will be. You could not ask for a better part or place from which to start than you currently occupy. So, read on and play like it means something to you!

I am the author and I have studied higher spiritualism for almost thirty years and for the last almost twenty years I have studied with The Council of Eight (the C8). I have been one of those present as the C8 has disseminated its 33 Grand Secrets of Spiritual Mysteries containing 158 Pearls of Wisdom one by one over a bit more than a period of six years. These teachings are quite helpful, and they can be found at www.grandsecretsofspiritualmysteries.com

MY AFFIRMATION AND DECREE FOR GS01-P001

"I am the door to unlimited prosperity and abundance and I am the wisdom that fills and illuminates my mind that I might know what to do next, that I may call forth from the Universe that which will insist upon helping me create this reality, that the doors of life might open before me, that I might step through into my prosperity and abundance, and that I may recognize, embrace and revel in it fully."

Feel free to visit the website and dig deeper when you are so inspired. This book came out of a conversation I had with Shugala, the head of the C8. Shugala has never been in physical form, but he speaks through quite a gifted channel. I had a mini stroke on 05/10/2019 (a 9 day in numerology) and I had a personal channeling with him on 08/11/2019 (a 22 day in numerology) where he suggested that perhaps I might want to write. He did not direct me in any way to write this book, but he seemed pleased with it when I asked for comments before submitting it to a publisher. I may have gotten some specifics incorrect, but he said, "Do not sweat the specifics." He is not prone to excess, so I took it all as high praise.

Anyhow, ascension requires both the mental and emotional bodies to be free of any attachments to that from which they are ascending, so to speak. The mental body will perceive what, how to, and why regarding moving to higher ground and the emotional body will focus its energy on the actual movement to higher ground. If the emotional body would like just one more taste of sex, money, and power, in this case, it will be drawn off course and the being will wind up reincarnating back in a sex, money, and power consciousness. No ascension will occur.

I have written two versions of When Penguins Fly. This one with my picture on the front as a 73-year-old will activate your mental body more than your emotional body. The other one with my picture on the front as a 6-year-old will activate your emotional body more than your mental body. You should read both books to get the full multibody experience.

SPIRITUAL BIOGRAPHY
June 04, 2024
1st Birth
Born September 18, 1950
Named John Lanaghan Craig

Born several weeks premature, I was left alone at hospital being fed intravenously fighting to be a viable Human Being. I was violently belt whipped by a father who was something of a rage-acholic and I ran out in front of a car sometime around the 4th of July 1956 while playing army hide and seek. I was crushed under the right front wheel too badly damaged for my Senior Beings to repair, so they truncated this timeline and took my six energetic bodies back in time to the moment of my birth and dropped them upon my emergent physical body at the quickening when the physical body takes its first breath. They did this because the energetic bodies never enter the physical body. The physical body in the womb is only that, it is not a Human Being. The six energetic bodies attach to various chakra locations upon the physical body and are the source of the aura which sometimes glows around the physical body.

2nd Birth
Born September 18, 1950
Named Andrew Patrick Timothy Michael Craig

My Senior Beings gave me this name. My father, on his death bed, told me he had no idea where the name came from. He asserted that he thought he had named me John Lanaghan Craig. Which, of course, he had done on the truncated timeline. Other than that, I was still born several weeks premature and left alone at the hospital being fed intravenously fighting to be a viable Human Being. Then I was violently belt whipped by a father who was something of a rage-acholic and I ran out in front of a car sometime around the 4th of July 1956 while playing army hide and seek. But my Senior Beings distracted the driver which gave me an extra two or three steps before the car hit me square in the face with its bumper and crushed out roughly half of my teeth and slammed me hard on the asphalt on my head and back. I was killed by cerebral hemorrhaging, but two lovely female arms reached out of the sky and wrapped my head in their hands bathing me in brilliant and overwhelming white light which healed my hemorrhaging and brought me back to the domain of the living.

Nothing Happens That Does Not Serve Some Purpose

So, what purpose did this twice lived 5 years and 9 months serve? What did these lives punctuated by extreme incidents of violence serve? They knocked the fifth dimensional consciousness I brought to the planet with me out of me so I could live a third and later fourth dimensional consciousness if I could get myself back to that level and they provided my Senior Beings with a source of direct experience of the highly unusual, from a Universe perspective, blight of "man's inhumanity to man" that seems to permeate every spec of the species of Human Beings upon this planet. My Senior Beings say that absent direct experience it simply cannot be understood by higher order beings. It has been a rough passage, but I believe I succeeded beyond expectations. And not a moment too soon for it is time for the movement to the 5DC to begin. Those that do not go to the 5DC with this Earth will be reassigned to other earth like planets around the Universe. So, step lively, yes? Yes!

The Remainder of My First 20 Years on The Planet Followed a Similar Path

It was a path with a very violent home life and additionally I began attracting that violence upon me in the outside world. I stayed small and almost malnourished to not provoke anyone but got beat up by older and bigger boys and was knocked out twice. Once with a broken left cheek bone and once which required an ambulance ride and 15 stitches in the back of my head and 8 stitches in my lip. I had a high IQ and graduated in the bottom 10% of my high school class. I moved into an apartment in college with some friends I made while in Corpus Christi for the summer doing Hurricane cleanup work. Four days after I moved in, they received a package in the mail, and it was from their friend in the army in Vietnam. It was a half-pound of marijuana from Vietnam. The police came just a short time later. Six months later I was in the Army in Germany driving tanks. I am proud of the Ukrainian's!

The Army Manned Me Up and My Next 20 Years Were Winning In The 3DC

I completed my undergraduate business degree with honors at Sam Houston State and my graduate business degree with honors at The University of Texas in Austin. I played rugby for five years and dated and then married a young lady that many of my friends thought to be the prettiest girl at Sam Houston State where we met. I went to work for Arthur Andersen & Co after graduation and after four years with them I went to work for Boone Pickens in Amarillo for a bit more than 7 years being the numbers man on an executive team generating the largest hostile takeover initiatives in corporate history at the time. Our efforts resulted in recapitalization of the assets of our target companies that added an additional $50 billion to their value when the DOW was at 2,000. The Dow is at 40,000 now so a comparable level of activity in the current economic environment would be somewhere around a $.5 trillion to $1 trillion increase in value. But when I was asked by my boss to move to California with him my wife refused to go, and I stayed with my family. Later I would learn that my wife had gone off the ranch on me in Amarillo and we got divorced. I decided that I had not come to win that game and began setting out on my spiritual journey. Bless her Heart!!!!!

I Attracted Failure in Every Business Endeavor I Started And Wasted Away Most Of My Prior Economic Gains

I felt like I was shedding a persona I had adopted to succeed in what to me was still a very hostile planetary existence. In 1995, I was led to the Aquarian Foundation and studied with Master Kumara, the Avatar of the 25,000 year long Aquarian age within which we still dwell and with the Brotherhood of Light and Ascended Masters of the Far East. Master Kumara passed on in 2000 and I left in 2005. Count Saint Germain was my Master Teacher while in the Foundation. Within a year of my leaving, I found my way to contact my Senior Beings and I remain deeply connected and committed to them. They are my family. I came here with them. I have uploaded all my experience with the blight of "man's inhumanity to man" and more and I have moved on from that project. They will process that understanding information and use it along with other information to reassign every Human Being that is either incapable of or does not want to go to the 5DC with our Mother Earth when she ascends there permanently. Currently you could say she is in limbo between dimensions. Bless her Heart!!!!!

In My Current Life I Am Working the Micro

I am working the micro in a similar but more invisible manner than the hostile takeover deals I did with Boone Pickens. I drive rideshare and I activate myself and my sacred objects into my vehicle as I drive and the sacred energies flow out into the Universe all around me. Into the grasses and flowers and bushes and trees and into the birds and the squirrels and the dogs and cats and horses and such. And even into the roads I drive upon and the buildings I pass as I drive. And I have driven more than 100,000 miles so far in 9,000 rides with certainly more than 10,000 people and perhaps as many as 20,000 people in my vehicle as I drive. And I teach as I drive. I say I call upon "All That Is Sacred in The Universe" to send me those that will inspire me and might be inspired by me and everything changes after I tell them that. I tell them that one must use a generous listening to actively listen for the inspiration or the opportunity to inspire and I distinguish it from the judgmental listening we have been trained in all our lives which just produces separateness and isolation and contributes so powerfully to the blight of "man's inhumanity to man". My riders open and share that which they might never have shared with anyone else before and we are laughing and laughing until the end of the ride. Many of them seem to realize there is an opportunity to heal something within their consciousness and spit it out to get it worked upon. There are others that are distracted and noncommunicative and I just drive but no one gets in my vehicle without being divinely blessed. Bless all my Riders!!!!!

I And My Senior Beings
Are Part of The Architecture of The Universe.

When Source created the Big Bang that resulted in the Universe, Source saturated the Universe with tiny particles of Source itself. These tiny particles, from the perspective of the Universe, are immortal and even Source has not been able to conceive of a means by which they might be destroyed. From the perspective of Human Beings, they represent our immortal souls. They are the recording agents so to speak of our lives and are fundamental to our experiencing and learning all that is available to be learned and experienced by Human Beings. And they are immortal so that Human Beings can live short lifetimes to learn specific lessons and then live about 3 times those lifetimes in spirit afterlife studying the lessons they were sent to learn and thereby completely learn those lessons. But Human Beings and the species itself can get intractably stuck in these lessons and so various Senior Beings were also created by Source to get stuck species of Human Beings unstuck. My Senior Beings observed alarming emissions from our Sun in 1945 after nuclear weapons were dropped upon Japan. So, they came to investigate and found that the Sun was preparing to kill every living thing upon the planet a thousand miles deep by wrapping the planet in a fist of coronal mass extrusion. The Sun is above all else the guardian of its solar system. My Senior Beings told the Sun to stand down and the Sun stood down but is still prepared to execute its plan if circumstances dictate. Bless our Sun for his poise and generosity!!!!!

From the very beginning of Human Beings in the Universe, My Senior Beings have been helping species of Human Beings, of which there are many, get unstuck. Prior to 2020, My Senior Beings have always used subtle influence techniques and practices to direct the species to the solution set to get itself unstuck. After 75 years of working in such a manner with this species of Human Beings they had achieved virtually no results and so they terminated that approach and they are now taking this planet, and those of her species of Human Beings that are enabled to go, to the 5DC by themselves. They have provided 33 Grand Secrets and 158 Pearls of Wisdom for those that would like to go to the 5DC. If one were to study one pearl each week it would take a bit over three years to study the material. For our team of Human Beings receiving the material originally it took over six years. It is in the Species Consciousness just from the act of our team of Human Beings receiving the information. But studying it is imperative for those that wish to go to the 5DC. And it seems reasonable to assume and would at least be prudent to assume that my Senior Beings will not need as much as 75 years to complete the ascension to the 5DC. In the interim they have advised us to ignore the bizarre behavior of Human Beings all over the planet right now because it is common for the Human Species to act out all sorts of bad behaviors when they are upon a planet, such as this one, that no longer is. The physical body of the planet is here but the energetic bodies of the planet are gone to higher ground now. And they are likely not ever coming back.

A Sweet Thing I Did for My Father
When He Died on December 02,2007

I went into ceremony with my mother, and I went into inner space to find him and there he was on a beautiful white stone pedestal table atop a lush Irish green grass hill with a bright white light blanket completely covering his physical form. I was on a lesser hill, and as I started into the valley between us, I noticed short little beings surrounding the hill just below the peak of the hill upon which my father lay in state so to speak. They had pillbox hats on and when they turned to me, they had massive teeth in their mouths shaped like triangles with sharp edges upon them. I took a knee, bowed my head, folded my forearms across my chest and blasted them with extremely bright white light and they were vaporized or otherwise disappeared. Then I flew down through the valley and up to my father and slid my arms under his form and turned flying down the hill into the darkness in the direction of his head upon the pedestal table. I was in the form of an archangel, and we flew into the pitch black below for a very long time until we came to a soft wall made of cloud material. I turned and flew straight up a great distance until at a certain level the band of clouds above us illuminated in a bright white light and two lovely female arms reached out to me and I placed the form of my father's body in the arms, they took him inside and the light went out. I retraced my path and exited inner space into my physical body with my mother sitting beside me. I told her the whole story of her husband's passage into the afterlife, and She was appreciative. The arms seemed to me the same arms that had healed my cerebral hemorrhaging when I was 5 years and 9 months old. All of this occurred after I thrice read a ceremony, I had written for him that affirmed and decreed that I would take him to the highest ground to which he would be entitled by any single deed he had done in his life. My Senior Beings attested to the accuracy of my description of the Heaven and Hell of the 3DC saying the blackness was the abyss from which my father might never have escaped, and the sharp toothed demons were the denizens of the abyss, and the beautiful white female arms were those of an angelic being joyfully receiving my father's form and soul from me. Two months later he had awakened and was told what I had done for him, and he contacted me through my Senior Beings to express his deep appreciation for what I had done for him. Twelve years later he contacted me through one of my female fellow travelers and gave me an excuse for why he beat me so much and it was at least a half-truth. But his not communicating through my Senior Beings suggests that more should or could have been said. I am nonetheless wholly at peace regarding the matter, and I dearly Love my father. Bless his Heart!!!!!

A Sweet Thing I Did on June 4, 2023

I was interviewed for a Podcast with Yaya Diamond, and I prepared this spiritual biography for that interview it was not until later that I realized what an interesting moment we had been drawn together to meet and speak with each other. On June 4, 2023, exactly one year prior to my interview I went to the memorial for the 26 Sandy Hook Elementary School children and staff that were murdered in Newtown Connecticut on December 14, 2012. I had written a ceremony intended to honor and heal them. There were 20 school children between the ages of 6 and 7 and 6 adult staff members murdered that day. I was not murdered but I overcame being killed twice at the age of 5 years and 9 months old. I thereby have a deep connection with them and so I activated a ceremony for them at their memorial by reading it aloud three times into existence. I have attached my ceremony for your review. I cried each time I read it. It was very moving to me. I rarely cry when I do ceremony, but I simply could not keep myself from crying, so I included that as a part of the ceremony. Bless their Sweet Hearts!!!!! Please read it thrice aloud to additionally activate it if you are so moved. And be sincere and loving as you do so or do not do it. Bless Your Heart!!!!!

Sincerely,
All My Love, My Loves, All My Love!!!!!
Andrew Patrick Timothy Michael Craig

MY SANDY HOOK CEREMONY
JUNE 04, 2023

BEAUTIFUL BLESSED AND BELOVED ONES
DWELLING IN SPIRIT FROM THE TRAGIC EVENT
AT YOUR SANDY HOOK ELEMENTARY SCHOOL

I AM – AND I AM THAT I AM
AND I AM THAT I AM
ANDREW PATRICK TIMOTHY MICHAEL CRAIG
BORN SEPTEMBER 18, 1950
IN PHILADELPHIA PENNSYLVANIA
I WAS CRUSHED UNDER THE RIGHT FRONT WHEEL
OF A CAR EARLY IN JULY OF 1956
ALMOST SIXTY-SEVEN YEARS BEFORE THIS DAY
AS I STAND IN YOUR MEMORIAL

I RAN OUT BETWEEN TWO PARKED CARS
THE MAN THAT KILLED ME COULD NOT STOP
SINCE MY HIGHER SPIRITUAL BEINGS
COULD NOT CHANGE THAT ON THAT TIMELINE
THEY WENT BACK TO THE INSTANT OF MY BIRTH
AND THEY REINITIATED MY TIMELINE
WITH MY CURRENT NAME BEING MY NEW NAME
AND WITH A SMALL GUST OF WIND ALLOWING ME
EXTRA STEPS BEFORE I WAS STRUCK BY THE CAR

ON THIS TIMELINE I WAS STRUCK IN THE MOUTH
BY THE BUMPER IN THE MIDDLE OF THE CAR
SLAMMED HARD TO THE GROUND AND
DRUG DOWN THE STREET PINNED UNDER THE CAR
AND MY HIGHER SPIRITUAL BEINGS WERE ABLE
TO RECOVER AND REACTIVATE ME
IT WAS ANOTHER 50 OR SO YEARS
BEFORE THEY SPOKE TO ME AGAIN
AS I FELT THEIR PRESENCE, I KNEW IT WAS THEM

I HONOR
THE GREAT COURAGE AND LOVE DISPLAYED
BY EACH OF YOU IN JOINING
THE TASK REQUESTED OF AND ASSIGNED TO YOU
AT SUCH AN EARLY AGE - YOU ARE MY HEROES
THE EARTH AND HER HUMAN BEINGS
ARE IN GREAT PERIL AT THIS TIME
YOUR PARTICIPATION IN THIS EXTENDED TIMELINE
IS FUNDAMENTAL TO IT BEING AVOIDED

WE ARE TAKING THE EARTH
AND CERTAIN OF HER HUMAN BEINGS
TO THE FIFTH DIMENSION OF CONSCIOUSNESS
AND YOU ARE HEREBY INVITED TO ASCEND WITH US
TO THIS HIGHER DIMENSION OF CONSCIOUSNESS
AND YOU ARE INVITED TO CONTACT
MY HIGHER SPIRITUAL BEINGS
FOR YOUR ASCENSION ENABLING TRAINING
IN SPIRIT

I DO NOT KNOW THE SPECIFICS
OF THE TASK YOU ACCOMPLISHED
WITH YOUR GREAT SACRIFICE
BUT YOUR PARTICIPATION IN THE EVENT
HAS ALL THE MARKINGS
OF A GREAT TASK ACCOMPLISHED
TO DISTINGUISH AND OVERCOME THE BLIGHT
THAT IS MANS INHUMANITY TO MAN
ON THIS PLANET

THE FIFTH DIMENSION OF CONSCIOUSNESS
IS ORGANIZED AROUND THE PRINCIPLES OF
LOVE, PEACE, HARMONY, TRANQUILITY, AND UNITY
THERE IS NO NEED FOR YOU TO RETURN TO
THE THIRD DIMENSION OF CONSCIOUSNESS
WHICH IS ORGANIZED AROUND THE PRINCIPLES

OF SEX MONEY AND POWER
AND WE SUGGEST THAT YOU NOT RETURN THERE
BUT IT IS YOUR FREE WILL CHOICE TO MAKE

LOVE AND LIGHT MY LITTLE ONES
I WENT INTO THE DARKNESS AT A VERY YOUNG AGE
BUT MY CONNECTION TO AND STUDIES WITH
MY HIGHER SPIRITUAL BEINGS ALLOWED ME
TO SEE HOW IMPORTANT IT WAS THAT I DID THAT
I AFFIRM AND DECREE THAT THOSE OF YOU
WHO DECIDE TO STUDY
WITH MY HIGHER SPIRITUAL BEINGS
WILL BE SIMILARLY REWARDED

SO, IT IS WRITTEN – SO IT IS SPOKEN – AND SO IT IS
APTMC – SUNDAY – JUNE 4, 2023

FIRST IMPRESSION

"Greetings, Beautiful, Blessed and Beloved ones from the spectacular Star Planet upon which we all joyfully dwell. I and my beloved are on the other side of the Universe equidistant from its center as we are on our side of it. I am upon a planet referred to by the species of Human Beings that dwell upon it as the Earth. I said I would stay connected, and this is me doing so. This is my First Impression.

I am known as Ninety-Nine and my beloved is known as Eighty-Eight here. We are on the Earth as we communicate with you. It is midnight sometime during their so-called "Year of our Lord" 2020. Certain of this species of Human Beings started time over when the Avatar of the Piscean Age came to teach them better behavior.

Well, that is, they did so after others of them had hung him on a cross and had him suffer in public and did a variety of other horrendous things to him before they allowed him to die. We suppose we should be glad they did not eat him.

The Earth is a truly beautiful planet perhaps designed and developed over a period of 4.5 billion years to house and cure certain Higher Order beings who would develop consciousness disorders. You would like it immensely if this species of Human Beings were not upon it. But perhaps they are the reason for her existence. It is a gateway planet housing a species of Human Beings of both the Third Dimension of Consciousness (3DC) and Fourth Dimension of Consciousness (4DC) which unfortunately often produces conflict between these beings.

But it is a planet configured as an ascension platform allowing its species of Human Beings to start at the 3DC, move up to the 4DC, and then ascend into the Fifth Dimension of Consciousness (5DC). With 3DC being full blown space and time Human Being consciousness, 4DC being the 3DC without the dark side, and 5DC being the first level of consciousness with dominion over space and time and or the world of matter as it were.

We view all of this with mirth because there does not seem to be agreement in this world of matter that consciousness can exist outside of matter. Scientists seem to think consciousness comes from the matter of their brains. Fortunately, being outside the world of matter, we can move at the speed of thought and instantly arrive anywhere we think ourselves. We use our imagination. And there is no resistance to movement in this world without matter, and we do not travel in the form of matter when herein either. So, there are no physical laws to prevent instant travel.

Prior to leaving our Star Planet, we released all matter, after reducing it to pure thought and when we arrived here, we remanifested our entire complex matter vehicles or bodies. But I digress. This is a planet previously referred to by Higher Order beings as the "Prison Planet and Insane Asylum of the Universe." Those same beings have now designated it as the "Greed Planet of the Universe."

The terms "Prison Planet" and "Insane Asylum" as used might be benignly referring to the repetitive looping of lifetimes in the 3DC. However, the addition of the term "Greed Planet" alters this entire reference in a major malignant direction.

So, congratulations, you Mother Earth Human Beings! You have hit the dark side trifecta even as you are incapable of seeing what a disaster you have become for the entire Universe! You exalt yourselves rather than expressing feelings of sorrow, regret, or remorse, or more. You are so incapable of perceiving the disaster you are, you expect us to celebrate you. Ha-ha! No!

Their Greed is just the worst. No single personality disorder of this species even bears mention when measured in units of profound destruction produced while present upon this planet. The Greedy can and are killing their planet, and potentially far beyond. In so doing, they have created this species as more of a monster on the loose than a species of Human Beings. All for their insatiable need, at every rotation of the planet, to take more than is theirs to take and to exalt themselves endlessly as better than all others.

Their Greed is always there in the low end 3DC. But this species failed to mature into high end 4DC humanitarians before their technologies posed a threat to the entire Universe and they refer with contempt to such high end 4DC Humanitarians, of which there are many.

They refer with contempt for the only members of their species that can save their souls from errors that could very well result in a permanent ban for them from reincarnating upon Planetary Beings ever again in this Universe. If they use thermonuclear weapons to kill even small numbers of Human Beings and completely innocent plants and animals, then those that do so and those that support them will likely be banned permanently from reincarnating upon any Planetary Being in the Universe.

I mean, what Planetary Being would allow them to live upon them after seeing what they did to their fellow travelers and to their Mother Earth. Not that the souls of those mauled and murdered by these weapons would be exterminated or extinguished. The "Source" that created the Universe did not create anything that can exterminate and extinguish the soul of a Human Being or a Planetary Being or a Solar Being.

At the Big Bang, Source exploded uncountable small particles of itself into the Universe which became the souls of sentient beings including the Human Beings and Planetary Beings and Solar Beings. Those that are killed by thermonuclear weapons will die a horrible physical death and will remember their deaths in detail in their souls. And Source will experience it also when the Big Suck occurs, as the souls come back to Source. Source will not be happy. This is not something Source wishes to experience.

Anyhow, events like this seem to require consequences that turn them into a cautionary tale. So, we are going to bless our Father Sun with these souls that no Planetary Being wants now. The ones that produced all the horrible deaths and those that supported them in anyway in doing that. At the start of their lives upon Father Sun their lives will be measured in intervals of less than a minute and there are so many of them that Father Sun will become known as a screaming Sun for some time to come. Human Beings and other sentient beings from all over the Universe will travel here to witness it directly. It cannot otherwise be understood."

So now we are openly upon their planet in action seeking to defuse the imminent devastation their unmatched, unique mix of Greed, Immaturity and Advanced Technology has produced. Words are entirely inadequate to convey the darkness of the pending events. And the Greedy would not help, even if they could understand the darkness of the events.

We have not been on their planet for long. We played peek-a-boo with the fighter jets as we were out over the northern oceans for a week or so when we first arrived. That was fun. The fighter pilots seek to be in command and to control the situation if one occurs. But we are above their pay grade, as they say, and they know it. Speed of sound vs speed of light anyone?

They refer to our craft as a "flying saucer." They think it is advanced technology. But it is just our Merkabah encasing our souls in exquisitely fine white light traveling at the speed of light.

They have so much they could learn from us but the Greed that infects them prohibits us from even informing them of the most obvious of truths available to us. They even have a saying for this aspect of their nature. They say, "No good deed goes unpunished." Yes, they are proud of it!

We draw energy directly from the fabric of the Universe and we never break down or even sleep. We are continuously awake and aware. We can travel through the Universe at the speed of thought, and yet, they speak with profound contempt for the only beings upon the planet with which we have any affinity.

Well, at least those whom they speak of with contempt will take a modicum of comfort, or more than that, from our presence upon the planet. Even if we are on a personal trip just now. Momentous changes are afoot. Their Mother Earth must ascend into the 5DC quickly. Otherwise, her Sun or some other threat will destroy her, and that threat could expand profoundly. We are not going to let that happen, as it would be the epitome of Evil. So, we have placed Mother Earth in a Cosmic Zip-Locked Baggie. We did not want to, but it was the only prudent thing to do.

We have already taken her to 5DC in the future but not one of her Human Beings came with her. So, we brought her back and moved back in time to allow for more ascension participants. She demanded that we bring all her species of Human Beings along, but they really must earn it. So, they need to get to work. She only gets one redo, and this is it so they should pay attention and their work will be easier to accomplish.

I suppose you can see her point of view. Going from eight billion Human Beings to zero in a single moment of consciousness must have been very shocking to her. Even if they were completely responsible for our having to do that. In our defense, this is the rarest of rare events. It is the first time a planet and at least some of her species of Human Beings will ascend concurrently. We had no known successful procedures to follow. And now that the cat is out of the bag, it has drawn interest from the farthest reaches of the Universe.

Since Mother Earth chose to come back for them the entire Universe is now aware of what we are doing before we do it and that has attracted many others not on our team. At this point, we are not sure what their intentions are, or the level of consciousness from which they have come. But they are from 5DC, and higher levels of consciousness and do not seem to be humored.

They are upon their own program, but it is at least likely to be consistent with ours, and we are working to protect Mother Earth and secondarily to fulfill her intentions as fully as possible. We typically adhere to a strict free will choice principle. But we have reviewed her history, and her species of Human Beings has quite recently devastated this planet on multiple occasions, and others had to fix it. So, we will be more initiative-taking this time.

The species of Human Beings upon the Earth have attracted the pending catastrophes that are requiring her rapid movement into the 5DC, and so, we have invited them to help lift her. Those of them who do help will move up into the 5DC with their Mother Earth, because that is her wish. But we say they must also drop the 3DC dark side to do so and, of course, no one will have to go to the 5DC with their Mother Earth. But if they do not go with her, they will go to another planet when she leaves. They will "be reassigned" and will have a permanent prohibition from returning to their Mother Earth. That would include whenever, if ever, they achieve 5DC.

The reassignment planets are like Mother Earth so they will be familiar with similar possibilities and potentialities available to them, and they may find themselves segregated by common beliefs or other commonalities also. Of course, there will be separate planets for the criminal, insane and greedy. They will all have taken that which was not theirs to take and so they will be temporary immortals long enough for them to be force fed every ounce of excess in which they have indulged. That is going to produce high drama and comedy. And they will live repeated lives on each of these three planets until they are completely purged of their dark side.

We consider this a profound gift for those that chose not to go to 5DC with their Mother Earth. They have engineered an epic catastrophe in a just few hundred years, so it is a gift! This rarest of rare events could also be described as the first time that a species of Human Beings has failed to ascend millions of years ahead of the ascension of their mother planet. So, it is not exactly the finest hour for her lads and lasses. However, their Mother Earth still loves them, and we similarly love her and so we will produce her request with small refinements.

We are not here to convince any of them to do the right thing. Doing the right thing does not need convincing. They know what the right thing to do is every time. It is just a choice and now would be an excellent time to choose to do the right thing at every opportunity! The Higher Order Beings upon the planet with us now can see every thought, action, and deed. Many of them are from dimensions of consciousness never touched upon by this species of Human Beings. They can see the entire conscious existence of every member of this species of Human Being at will. Nothing is private. These Higher Order Beings will see every lie and dishonorable thought, action, and deed. Again, it is time for this species of Human Beings to do the right thing every time.

Even the purest and the best and brightest of these Human Beings keep libraries of secrets. But there are no secrets at the levels of consciousness of these Higher Order Beings. They are above the 5DC and may even extend up into the 11DC. Those of this species of Human Beings who have big secrets will have quite a bit more work to do than those with just your average embarrassing thoughts, actions, and deeds that they wish to keep secret.

The complete impossibility of erasing any of that in the near term will be very confronting. This species understands that Spacetime is (x, y, z, t). However, they do not have any notable knowledge concerning dimensions of consciousness. The dominant view is that consciousness is created by the cells and energies of brains, so they think it is private and inaccessible to others. The error of that view of consciousness is going to be a stunning awakening

For instance, I could say, to the average person on the street, that the 3DC includes a full range of negative thoughts, actions, and deeds, and the 4DC has, at least, far less negativity, and the 5DC includes dominion over space and time and the 3DC and 4DC do not. I could add that the 5DC includes an unparalleled level of positivity. Simple concepts, and yet, the average person would gaze upon me with a blank stare, at best.

Or I could speak to the existence of 5DC and even higher order beings without form that communicate through 4DC human beings using their bodies as vessels for communication, and I might be met with a harsher response than a blank stare. Because none of this exists in their libraries or schools, or sciences anywhere. They really must go off the so-called grid to acquire this type of information, and few have the interest required to find and flourish within this sort of information.

Or I could tell them that Human Beings do not ascend from the 3DC because the negative stuff is a deal killer, and I think most of them could easily understand that in the way in which they understand such things. I mean, they seem to know lying and killing and everything in between is wrong to do, and it makes them sinners who will have to pay in the afterlife.

But, when I would tell them that Human Beings can only ascend from the 4DC, the dimension they speak of with contempt, well as they would say "them is fighting words." Then we would see what I mean when I say having both 3DC and 4DC on the same planet at the same time often causes conflict. Ha-ha!

Better yet, when I have sought to explain the 5DC, I have said that in the 5DC, this species of Human Beings is a single organism with each Human Being both independent of and attached to each other as one. I am fortunate I can move at the speed of thought. So, I told them they might refer to that as kind of a "Quantum Entanglement" and sufficed it to say that in 5DC you never really walk alone. I do not think they knew what that was, so they just nodded in agreement.

As we have said, we are working to protect Mother Earth and to fulfill her intentions. But in addition, we are looking to enrich the rest of the Universe. We submitted an enrichment project to Mother Earth and our Star Planet, and all parties have approved it. So, if you would like to observe or even participate, feel free to stay connected to our consciousness. We are heading to the land down under to Melbourne, Australia."

"Star Planet Expeditionary Mission Control here! Ninety-Nine, are you and Eighty-Eight safe? Eighty-Eight, are you and Ninety-Nine safe? Come in, come in, come in!

That sounds like a nightmare! Are there any similar Planetary situations of which you are aware on that side of the Universe? It is little more than a pure accident that you found this situation! Come in, come in, come in! Do you need help?"

"Hey, hey Mission Control! Ninety-Nine here! Eighty-Eight Here too! Everything is within spec, so to speak, so we are good!"

"We are absolutely staying connected to your consciousness! We have listening crews ten deep back here. We are reporting to the planet every day on multiple occasions. At times, the whole planet seems to stop to listen to your musings!"

"You are too kind, Mission, too kind! Thank you! We are here representing the whole planet and it is important to us that you keep us trued up so to speak if we waver. It is a challenging environment of mixed consciousnesses. It is difficult to explain but we may need truing up from time to time. Thanks! Ninety-Nine and Eighty-Eight out!"

"Got it! Mission out!"

OUR ENRICHMENT PROJECT

Eighty-Eight and I saw an article about a pair of Fairy Penguins in Australia. We came across a picture of the pair, and we thought, Love and Light. We saw an aged female with a young male seeming to comfort her in the picture and the vivid colorations of the soul energies surrounding each and both was a remarkable sight. Both radiant and soft whites, blues, pinks, greens, and yellows. We contacted a woman there that is 4DC and is familiar with the pair and their Colony.

Oh yes, the little Penguins have souls. As do all the members of the so-called animal kingdom upon this planet. And like the Human Beings, all their energetic bodies are outside of their "Physical Body." The energetic bodies, the "Mental Body," the "Soul Body," the "Spiritual Body," the "Emotional Body," the "Vibrational Body," and the "Astral Body," surround the Physical Body of the Human Beings like layers of an onion. Five of these bodies connect to the Physical Body at small chakra points and the Soul Body connects to the Physical Body indirectly through the Spiritual Body. And the Soul Body is the outer layer of the onion, yes?

The Soul Body stays separate from the Physical Body on this planet because it is immortal and everything on this planet experiences life as profoundly limited into, at best, segments of aliveness punctuated by stark beginnings and endings. The Soul Body is the immortal aspect of consciousness which allows the Earth Human Being to lift into higher dimensions of consciousness over its many segments of aliveness and it does that in part by maintaining only indirect contact. My love and I can attest to the strength of the dominant beginnings and endings concept on this planet! It is just horrible!

The fetus in the womb of the Human Being is just the emerging Physical Body and it draws its energy entirely from its astral chakra around the area where it is attached to the mother's body with the umbilical cord. Once born, the energetic body known as the Astral Body will attach to the Physical Body in this area. The area of the belly button.

Upon leaving the body of its mother, at the quickening, when the Physical Body takes its first breath and becomes a Human Being, all the energetic bodies attach to chakras on the Physical Body as noted above and the Physical Body begins drawing its energy from its third eye chakra located in the middle of its forehead where the Spiritual Body attaches to it.

Given that the Soul Body does not even touch its own Physical Body and that all the other energetic bodies only touch this Physical Body at small chakra points upon the Physical Body, it is inconceivable that any of them would imbed themselves deeply inside the Physical Body of the mother of the Human Fetus to attach to that Human Fetus indirectly or just barely. Yet, there are laws here that make aborting a Human Fetus akin to murdering a Human Being, which a Human Fetus is not, and they thus override the intuitive consciousness of the life giver for the Human Fetus and that override has allowed for souls banned from this Planet to reenter the Planet and create additional chaos and destruction.

For a Penguin, the umbilical cord attaches the fetal body inside the egg to the yolk of the egg, upon which it feeds, and when the fetus gets big the body cracks the egg open and takes its first breath.

The nine months for a Human Fetus to mature to viability are also a test track for the functionality of the Physical Body. If any vital systems poorly evaluate the Physical Body of the mother spontaneously aborts the Human Fetus and it does not leave the womb capable of living.

As is so for Penguins. The time in the egg, the external womb if you will, for the Penguin Fetus, is also a test track for the functionality of the Physical Body. If any vital systems poorly evaluate, the Penguin Fetus does not leave the egg capable of breathing life into itself. Or, if the caretaking Penguin abandons the egg for any reason the Penguin Fetus does not leave the egg capable of breathing life into itself.

Of course, there is a reason for all of this. As previously stated, the shell of the Soul Body is the Merkabah. So, the soul must be external to the Physical Body in order that the being may time travel etc. Furthermore, at higher levels of consciousness, the Soul Body must be external to the Physical Body in order that the truth of an individual may always be available in the instant of need, yes? So, perhaps you can see a bit deeper why we were so enamored with the little Penguins. They radiated Love and Light and they were completely without guile of any sort.

It is with great pleasure, Mission Control, that now we introduce you to our Penguins. They are adorable and hysterical. It is hard to not love them. They sort of crawl up inside your heart and set up residence there."

"You have our complete attention, Ninety-Nine!"

We are sitting beside the pair of Penguins across the water from Melbourne, Australia. They do not notice us. We are so still; they cannot even see us when they look directly at us. It is a very still and lovely night. Clear sky, sparkling stars and city lights and various noises coming across the water from the civilization located there.

An hour or so has passed before we speak. We say, "How are you feeling?" And they look at each other and both say, "Just as happy as I could ever hope to be." Then they look at each other puzzled and begin dissecting the conversation to see where it seemed to go wrong. And, we say "That was us asking that question."

The young male is looking over her shoulder and he sees us and almost jumps out of his skin and his sudden alarm sets her off and she turns and sees us and falls on her back screaming. She is holding her chest screaming "It's my heart, it's my heart!!!" We are rolling on the ground laughing and the little guy is menacing us saying "That is not funny man!" Oh, but he is so wrong. That is funny! And then he stops and asks us "How is it I understand you and I am speaking back to you in your tongue?" And she jumps up and says, "Yeah?"

"We are glad to see you have gotten over your heart problem! That was funny! But let me introduce myself and my better half, yes? We are a 5DC Human Being. I am the male principle, and she is the female principle of our being, and we are from the other side of this Universe. And while you may perceive us as two, we are more like a single being and the same would be said if there were two billion of us. We are a species that has perfected unity and having separate bodies is integral to our unity and a matter of convenience.

"When on planets not our own I go by the moniker of Ninety-Nine (99) and she goes by Eighty-Eight (88) or vice versa and unless otherwise overruled either now or in the future we are going to call the two of you Lady Master Light and Master Love. We assume from your joy, that will work for you. You can speak with us because we have expanded your intellect to know our language as well as we know it. You are listening and speaking from a new brain if you will. It is temporary."

"But Lady Master Light and I have beaks. How can we even make the sounds we are making without lips? Even more than that, how is it that we now know all this new information?"

"Like we said my friend, it is temporary, but it might become permanent if you moved to our planet. You all picked up on it right away, except for Lady Master Light and her Heart, yes?"

"Now, now, Sir! That is a time-honored defense mechanism. You get them laughing long enough for someone to save you or something like that and I am saved and so I rest my case! So, do you have room service and maids and all of that at your planet? We have been to some mighty fine places so I would not go half-stepping on us. Isn't that right Junior?"

"Yeah, what she says. And I think you are supposed to call me the Master of Love now Sugar. I mean I cannot help it if word has started getting around. When you are good it gets known."

"Please! Everyone knows you cannot start talking up these young ones. It goes to their head and nothing but trouble after that. He said Master Love, Junior, not Master of Love."

"Where did he say you were from Eighty-Eight? Was it the other side of Melbourne or across the ocean or somewhere in the up over or something like that?"

"Lady Master Light, you are Hysterical. Ninety-Nine said from the other side of the Universe. Way past the Sun and the Moon and the Galaxy and you can only get there at the speed of thought."

"Well, I hope we will not be traveling there at the speed of Juniors thought. Ha-ha! Although he did seem quick witted renaming himself the Master of Love. Ha-ha!"

"I knew you would start warming up to my new moniker, Lady Master Light. I think I may get me a couple of those T-shirts. Say black fabric with "The Master of Love" in white letters on them."

"You guys are so sweet to each other. Ninety-Nine and I thought it might be, but we were not sure. Have you heard about reincarnation? It is where a being dies and then is reborn in another body. It usually takes around three times the number of years the being lived in the physical before they reincarnate into the physical and begin life anew. But some take a short cut.

The Buddhists have a ceremony they call PHOWA which they say allows their adherents to reincarnate in 45 days or less and for Penguins it might be only a fraction of that. Also, non-Buddhists can enact similar ceremonies with similar results. The fundamental driver is the devotees desire to return rapidly and commitment that they will do so. And, if there are two beings that just terribly miss each other when one is suddenly killed the sheer power of their intent to be together might allow quick reincarnation also."

"Eighty-Eight is tight and right on all that Lady Master Light. But, of course, then you have the problem that they are not the same age and everything. But that is a small bridge to cross compared to crossing the gulf between the living and the dead."

Suddenly, everything gets still. Like life itself stops for this moment. The air is still with no lights flickering and no city noises. I look at Eighty-Eight and she looks at me. We hold our breath. "What have we done?" Lady Master Light stands there staring at Master Love, and he hangs his head and shuffles his feet.

Then she says "Earnest, is that you in there?"

Master Love says, "Well it used to be Ruby, but I have changed."

Eighty-Eight says, "Okay, Great! Reunion is over and we can just get to work, right?" But they pay us no mind.

Ruby takes a few steps and launches herself at old Earnest knocking him to the ground. She is on top of him head butting him in the beak and trying to choke him with her flippers. We are trying to pull her off, but she is firm in her intent to do him in.

She is yelling at him, "The only thing good about you and that Floozy Lucille is the fact that the Leopard Seals ate both of you. Did she reincarnate with you too?"

"Heavens no, baby! Heavens no! I just made a bad mistake. You know how I can get filled up with myself. Well, that happened, and I made a bad mistake and I got killed. I am so sorry. But against all odds, I came back to be with you because I Love you and I am here to accept my punishment and I will even wear the white T-shirt with Dumb Bell in black letters on it."

"No, no, no Earnest! We are going to have to adjust and go back to being the wonderful little pair the rest of the Colony knows us as. And how are we going to fix this now, Boss?"

"Let me take this Ninety-Nine. Lady Master Light, you could both die at the same time and stick together that way or you could each live and die in the ordinary course of life and meet up on the other side and reincarnate together."

"How about if I terminate him and put a homing beacon on him and send him back now while letting him know that I will be along shortly, and he better be available when I show up?"

"Yeah, we do not think it works that way, Lady Master Light. It is a free will choice thing, and we would consider your terminating him a termination of the attraction of the relationship for him."

"Okay, Miss Boss! I am going to take Junior with me, and we are going to bed down and sleep a bit. This whole thing has straight up worn me out."

"And that is how it works Lady Master Light. You are the wisdom and Master Love is the passion. You are the mind, and he is the

ANDREW PATRICK TIMOTHY MICHAEL CRAIG

heart. And Love and Light are the fabric of the Universe. And do not talk about this my Luvs. They will think you are crazy!"

"Yeah, I agree with you on that point Miss Boss! I am starting to think I am a crazy too! We have been moving at high velocity, shall we say even for someone like yourselves, and we are not even human beings, so I am touch and go on the point at any moment in time. But I appreciate your keeping me from doing harm to my Earnest. He is still the love of my life! But let us keep that between us, yes?"

"Will do, Lady Master Light! Will do!"

THE SPHERE

"Hey, Mission Control over here. We are laughing and crying over here. Bring the Penguins back with you Luvs! Bring them back with you! And, oh yes, be especially safe now!"

"Thanks for the encouragement, Mission! Eighty-Eight and I are getting close to those two. They are just so authentic and adorable we want to hug them all the time!"

"Ninety-Nine, see if you can locate and acquire the Sphere that traveled outside of space and time. Your observation of it and the unexpected nature of it emerging from a Mother Earth planet is the primary reason you are there. Remember?"

"Mission, mission, mission! Now you are not supposed to get ahead of us. It is hard enough dwelling in the drama storm that is this planet and its people without your getting ahead of us and suggesting we are off pace. Be assured we are moving at high velocity. Ask our Penguins. We appreciate your concern but please do not lean on us."

"Ruby and Earnest have gone back to the colony to sleep with their mates for the night and Eighty-Eight and I were about to go into meditation and summon the Sphere to us. It seems like it has almost a planetary consciousness so we should be able to communicate with it easily. It will provide shelter, safety and comfort for our travels, training, and study."

"I am 100% with Ninety-Nine on that. It is easy and effortless for us to travel in our combined Merkabah, but I would never take our little Penguin friends off planet without the Sphere. And we are not even close to leaving but the Sphere will certainly impress them and give us some private training space. So, excuse us as we commence meditating."

Oooooooooom! Oooooooooom! Oooooooooom!

"There we go. Nicely done, Eighty-Eight!"

"I expected it to be full size, Eighty-Eight, but it adjusts to the number of parties either already in it or about to enter it. So, it is in a hot rod configuration just for we two now. I will inform it that we are a party of two hundred and see what it does."

"Wow! That was an upgrade. It looks like a space liner now. And it has opened a door for us. How nice is that. Please my Love, let it be that you are the first to set foot in it."

"Only if you hold my hand and step in right behind me, Ninety-Nine. We do not know if it is occupied already or if there is some other factor in there that is dangerous to us."

"Point well taken on this planet, Eighty-Eight. Point well taken. But this is a vehicle not of this planet. Its materials are not known on this planet and the software which animates the vehicle is even more distant from this planet than the materials. Quite an exotic vehicle. I am impressed."

"It appears this vehicle could take all of us and more to our Star Planet. Higher Order beings must have helped the Human Being. It is way too advanced in design, materials, and construction for his dimension of consciousness. He did something to have them help him, so we must give him credit for that. Additionally, there appears to be an open authorization from the Human Being that invented it that Higher Order Beings may use it when in need on the condition that they return it in good order when done with it. How precious is that? He has conditions!" Ha-ha!

"So, we will use the Sphere, Eight-Eight. The Human Being that created it traveled back roughly 75 years in time to a time even before his own birth to address certain Humans Beings that numbered in the hundreds of thousands then and more now. It is an efficient structure with a smaller Sphere in the center that is a stage, and optics that allow everyone to see the stage head on without regard to their location within the Sphere. It can expand to hold millions or contract to hold just two."

"Certain Higher Order Beings granted the man the opportunity to change any one thing he would choose to change. He chose to change the Atomic Bombs that the United States dropped on Japan in WWII. He did that because he had learned that Nuclear Fusion exterminates the souls of 3DC and 4DC Human Beings. And these bombs killed one hundred thousand Human Beings instantly and two hundred thousand or more over the next few months."

"He was sad because these souls were part of the God consciousness distributed at the Big Bang. It seemed to him the worst harm that Earth Human Beings had ever visited upon the Universe and so he set out to correct it. He and two Archangels that accompanied him while traveling in this Sphere snatched the Atomic Bombs just before they dropped, and they threw them into the Sun while replacing them with comparable plastic explosives. The plastic explosives crushed Japan's desire to continue the war just as well as the Atomic Bombs and the man and Archangels deleted that use of atomic weapons against Human Beings. It did not happen."

"The Sphere was set up prior to the atomic bombing and the man and Archangels coded the DNA of the three hundred thousand and more Human Beings to have them leave the cities whenever there was a war. The intention being for them to avoid the plastic explosives also. Once coded the three hundred thousand Human Beings went back in time to the moment of their birth, and they lived their lives again and they avoided the plastic explosives also. There were very few that died upon the event of the replacement bombs that the United States dropped on Japan. You could count them on your hands."

"Over time, the replacement bombs dropped by the United States on Japan will process throughout Earth history and be a permanent part of the planetary consciousness. To date it is in its infancy and is only known by Higher Order Beings. But unbeknownst, at the time, to the one that changed it, those atomic bombs were crude fission weapons. And those crude fission weapons did not exterminate any souls of Human Beings. Still, the saved souls that passed later from old age Love him."

"And those that were in the cities at the time of the plastic bombs have reported no uniquely bad deaths. Their deaths were like falling and hitting their heads or something. Just turn out the lights, yes? However, the subsequent testing of open-air nuclear fusion bombs attracted the "Solar Being." And the Solar Being does not allow nuclear fusion, not its own, within its planetary system. And prior to our arrival he was intending to wrap the Earth in a fist of Coronal Mass Extrusion that would exterminate every living thing upon or within it up to a thousand miles deep."

"As of this moment the Solar Being has paused his reaction to the fusion weapons. In the event he eliminates this pause then catastrophic will be an insufficient word for the result. And now certain of the Earth Human Beings have developed nuclear fusion energy devices with sustained temperatures of 75 million degrees Celsius peaking at 100 million degrees Celsius. They say these are temperatures five times hotter than the core of the Solar Being. If there is an accident the Solar Being will know. And even if there is not an accident there may be some sort of emissions that will alert the Solar Being. Or if there is a war the facility will be targeted and who knows what happens when a fusion reactor is hit by a missile with a thermonuclear warhead on it. Yikes! So, the situation remains delicate. The Earth Human Beings have provoked their own destruction and seem incapable of even perceiving it let alone correcting for it."

"Ninety-Nine, just what the heck are we doing on this planet anyway? I have listened to your musings. Just how is access to these weapons and technologies controlled. What are our risks? Might they bomb us? Have we set up protection and escape mechanisms? Have we done time and motion analysis to determine the time we need to escape pending events? Have we thought about just telling them to stand down? Are we handcuffed? Are we expected to risk our own extermination to avoid upsetting them?"

"I am sorry, I went off in a bit of a trance there. We have taken certain measures Eighty-Eight, and we are attempting to resolve this entire debacle in rough terms in accordance with Mother Earth's wishes. Their Mother Earth thinks of them as her precious children, and she is their mother. Planets do not get around much so you can see her point of view. If she would meet Human Beings from other planets, she might be mad at hers. I would be."

"In the interim, we will use the Sphere for our project here. It is an honor to piggyback on that event! My remote viewing of that event is why we are here. To your point, Eighty-Eight, at one point they had more than eighty thousand such weapons, but they almost got into a nuclear war, and so they eliminated most of those weapons and there are now below fifteen thousand such weapons. But they are newer, more sophisticated, and destructive weapons. So, I am not sure the net peril to the Earth has declined much. And the nation with the largest population is now increasing its nuclear weaponry which will trigger a new arms race."

"However, consider this - the standard tactical thermonuclear bomb of the United States, the B61, is a variable yield tactical weapon with its maximum yield somewhere around the explosive equivalent of seven hundred fifty thousand pounds of TNT. And a single pound of TNT detonated in a crowd could kill a hundred people or so. That is just one tactical bomb out of those fifteen thousand or so weapons noted above which also include much larger strategic weapons. So why would they need another arms race? There is risk, but it is manageable, and it will not manifest into any harm to anyone or anything. So, let us set that aside and give it no further thought, yes? I hear Penguins!"

"Boss and Miss Boss!! Is this your spaceship? Master Love and I have been up for hours. We could hardly sleep. Tell us about everything. We are so excited. We are beside ourselves!"

"Whew! That must have been both of you yelling but I could not distinguish separate voices. Did something happen last night?"

"Indeed, it did, Boss, indeed it did! We figured how to think and speak and even move as a single unit. Unbelievable! Do you do that with your mate, Boss?"

"Well, Eighty-Eight, is more like an aspect of us than being a mate of mine. I am not sure there is an equivalent of a mate in 5DC. It might appear as such, externally, but not in inner space. In inner space, we sort of process off a Colony Mind, like you do, but it is vastly expanded compared to yours. But our souls are separate, so that every one of us might contribute our unique creativity with 5DC integrity to our sort of Colony Mind."

"For us, it seems like the best of both worlds. The worlds of the collective single organism and the creative individual. But it does take a bit of training to be able to manage your thoughts in a manner that is always effortlessly polite and respectful."

"The so called "lesser" beings of this species of Human Beings will love the genuine equality and epic emancipation that is a fundamental aspect of the 5DC. They will have to let go of things, but their "betters" will find it all much more difficult!"

"You two are a remarkable tribute to the 5DC creativity of your species. Perhaps you would like to teach it to other members of your Colony. Let's have a Big Spirit Party with performers and singing and dancing. Who are your dancers?"

"Well, of course, Master Love and I are dancers. There are maybe another hundred or so that I am sure would do it. But it could be more than that if they get the mind expanders."

"Let us start with ninety-five and work from there, Lady Master Light. We will need seven stagehands and forty-four young performing couples, and with the four of us that makes ninety-nine in total."

"Alright, we are having a party! I am telling Paula, Priscilla, and Penelope first. They are my sisters, and they love dancing. And they love their men too! And Master Love will get you his strongest and hardest working friends, Boss. We will be back with our friends soon! And we are going to go to lunch with the Colony before we come back."

"Make sure you watch out for the Leopard Seals Master Love!"

"I am going to smack you Ninety-Nine! Lady Master Light is sensitive to the whole Leopard Seal debacle and Master Love is even more so. How about giving them a little space. He came back for her which is very romantic. So, you be nice, or I will smack you right in front of them."

"Now, now, now Eighty-Eight, you know how much I love you smacking me around in public, but we do not want to set a bad example for the kids, yes? So please try and restrain yourself."

"I know, you are cracking yourself up, right Ninety-Nine?"

"Indeed, I am Eighty-Eight! Indeed, I am! Humor just might be the hidden gem of the numerous species upon this planet."

"You are incorrigible, Ninety-Nine! They seem so enthusiastic to me. And remarkably coherent too. I mean they went from never having spoken to speaking this Human language better than most Human Beings. You need to give them some credit!"

"It makes them more comfortable Eighty-Eight. They figure the jokes at their expense means there is nothing to worry about. It is a subliminal background language so to speak."

"Okay, enough! You win! Filter yourself now if you can. I am just honored to be a custodian of theirs. They are so authentic. What you see is what you get. What a relief. the Human Beings on this planet are so dishonest and hateful that I am sort of in awe of our little penguin friends Ninety-Nine."

"I cannot imagine that they are not all aboard Eighty-Eight, but it will take some time to get them up to standard to participate in the type of party for which we are renowned, yes?"

"Ninety-Nine! You are really begging me to smack you aren't you! These are our little babies. So, let us just start preparing them for their future and not for the Big Spirit Party. We have had many parties before, but we have never born a new species before. I do not think anyone from our planet has ever done this before so I need a few moments from time to time to be overwhelmed by it if you will."

"Okay! Okay! You oversee the esoteric, so to speak? And I will oversee the pace. I am sort of like Earnest in a way. I have not been immortal that long and so I am still good at providing pace which is something which is vital to this initiative. Yes?"

"Hey, Mission Control here! We want to make sure there is no smacking around in front of the kids! Okay? We think it might create some bad habits from this otherwise idyllic species. Hello! Hello! Mission Control here!"

"Okay, okay Eighty-Eight here and no smacking around. Got it! It may be that we are catching a bit of Earth Humor which would perhaps not be funny on our Star Planet."

"Oh contraire, Eighty-Eight, we are rolling on the floor and smacking each other around over here so we recommend you all cease that potential activity immediately. Or we might have to smack you around when you get back, right?

"Sounds like you are covering for Ninety-Nine, Mission Control. But I will not smack him in front of them. Out!"

"I am going to set the cloaking Eighty-Eight. I will be right back."

"Are you with me Mission?"

"Yes, Ninety-Nine. Just doing a little truing up. Ha-ha! Out!"

"Great, thanks for the truing up, Ninety-Nine out!"

THE TEAM EXPANDS

Here come our Penguins and their special friends back from lunch. These will be our partners in this great affair. I signal Ruby and Earnest to have their friends bow their heads. And I initiate the intellect upgrade that we had originally done with Ruby and Earnest and when we all raise our heads, and I say, "How do you all feel" the whole crew sort of falls apart. Bless their hearts!

This is an enormous leap in intellect and consciousness, and some are laughing, some are crying, and some are just incredulous. But before they go completely over the edge Ruby and Earnest step in and tell them "Everything is okay."

"My fellow penguins! Listen up! I am the one you have known as Ruby my whole life. And that which has just occurred within you occurred for me several days ago and it will change our lives forever. Boss over here and his lady say it is temporary. But I do not know how it could possibly be temporary."

"For instance, the young male with me today is the reincarnated spirit of my Earnest. He missed me terribly after the Leopard Seals ate him and he missed me so much he quickly reincarnated to come back to my side. How can that be temporary?"

"Until Boss and Miss Boss gave us the intellect upgrade, we could not even think or understand such thoughts let alone manifest them. It was all beyond us. But now, it is mostly second nature to us, and we discover new things every day. And I figure it is a gift from which I and we cannot back down. And if it is only temporary, I do not want it to be said that was because we or I failed to honor and manifest it at every turn. So, when Boss and Miss Boss said they will host a "Big Spirit Party" if we could get more of us, we picked you. We did so because we love you and respect you deeply. And we did so because we knew you would not back down and be small. We knew you would play to win and that you would win. And so, this is our gift to you, and you are our gift to ourselves!"

"You are aware that your intellect is dramatically expanded and if you chose to participate with us, you will also undergo dramatic changes in your body and every other aspect of you and yet, Miss Boss has assured us that we will remember everything prior to our entering this event and we will find that our world will expand dramatically but not beyond our abilities. Our abilities will always stay a step ahead of our need for them all the way up to as high as we go. And that could be quite high. But what the heck, does anyone have a better offer?"

"Thank you, Ruby! You all can speak, you know. So, if you have a better offer speak up. Yeah, us too! Just freaking speechless but it will pass soon. Ruby and Earnest are like professors in just a few days. Eighty-Eight and I hold them both in the highest regard. They are champions! How about if you all go discuss it on our own, okay. This can be intimidating right out of the air. So, you all go have a chat and let us know who is in and out."

"Off they go, Ninety-Nine. Lady Master Light really showed some leadership there. I was about ready to start rallying myself. But I held back, it really is their decision to make. How many do you think will join in anyhow?"

"Ha-ha! All of them Eighty-Eight. This is a necessary formality at this point but every one of them is already sold on the deal! And here they come."

"Welcome back everyone! Thank you for joining us in our travels. We have brought a magical Sphere with us to assist in our travels and it will also serve as a school and a training ground for you so let us go inside and get a feel for it. Oh yes, it is cloaked so do not be surprised at the size of it when I turn the cloaking off so that we may enter it."

"There it is! Impressive, yes? And it is even more impressive inside. Once inside, I will cloak it again, so we are not disturbed."

"That is beyond bigger than big and so shiny and beautiful, Boss. I thought Ruby was exaggerating when she spoke about it being better than a fine hotel, but this would top them."

"And you are?"

"I am Priscilla, Boss and Miss Boss. Thank you for everything!"

"Well Miss Priscilla, Eighty-Eight and I are equally impressed with and thankful for your participation. Your Ruby speaks very highly of you and your sisters."

"Everybody, listen up now. I will be your gymnastics coach. You will have a tremendous transformation in your physical body, and you will need training in how to move it around with skill and grace so to speak. And gymnastics is a great place to start learning that. It will grant you strength and flexibility even as you learn of such limits as your new body is subject to."

"Eighty-Eight will be your ballet coach. It is a form of dance that is very formal and classic and elegant. It is a very nice complement to gymnastics. It takes the profoundly competent physical body achieved from the gymnastics, and transforms it into moving, flowing artistry."

"Just before we begin doing this you will be growing a new body. It will have long legs, and arms with elbows and wrists and hands, and the hands will have fingers and an opposable thumb. It will have wings that are imbedded within the upper back that are extremely strong and light weight and twice your height, which will be either three, four or five feet tall. In addition to just learning how to function in your new body you will also need to learn to fly. We have never done what you are about to do, so we will help, but we may have little idea of what is confronting you at any point in time. You will need to show some patience with us at times also."

"You will be able to shape shift in and out of your new body with your current penguin body being the other presentation of yourself. You will rarely do that while inside the Sphere because every movement in your new body is important right now."

After teaching you Ballet, Miss Boss will teach you a whole array of modern dance, including tap dancing, which is a favorite of mine. These dances will grant you a certain hip cat sort of finesse on the dance floor. This will be so much fun for you all, that you will do it just for play, so to speak. So, first is a new body with body building exercise and then an array of dancing lessons, and then we will move on to singing and playing musical instruments. We will also study mathematics and science and art and other academic interests as you may find you are drawn to."

"If we were training a Human Being child in lengths of time, this training would take a decade or two. But inside this sphere, we are not in lengths of time. So, when we leave the Sphere, no more than a few hours in lengths of time will have passed and it will go by effortlessly and enjoyably. Eighty-Eight will now show you where your quarters are. See you in the morning!"

"Come on my babies the living quarters are in the back, and they are very comfortable. We will start with a single room. The rooms are very flexible so whatever your sleeping customs are the room will conform to your needs. Okay!"

"And the room will assign you numbers based upon its assessment of you, but it will do so while you sleep. When you awaken your number will be upon your night shirt. We will discuss those further in the morning, but I will say a little about the numbers tonight so that you will not fret about them."

"Over the millennia, Human Beings have sought to identify external indicators about themselves and each other allowing them access to unique wisdoms. One of these systems relies on translating names, dates and words into numbers and then revealing the wisdom resonant within the numbers. In evaluating the numbers one through ninety-nine, nine of them are doubles. They are the 11, 22, 33, 44, 55, 66, 77, 88 and 99."

"The 11, 22 and 33 are Master Numbers. The 44, 55, 66, 77, 88 and 99 are Power Numbers. These numbers are not reduced. However, all the other numbers are reduced to a single digit. A 23 would be 2+3=5 and a 32 would be a 3+2=5, and a 97 would be a 9+7=16=1+6=7 and a 79 would be a 7+9=16=1+6=7. That is except for the eight two-digit numbers that reduce to an 11. The numbers 29, 38, 47, 56, 65, 74, 83 and 92 reduce to an 11 and then the 11 is not further reduced."

"There will only be eighteen final numbers at most. There will be some combination of the nine duplicate numbers and the nine single digit numbers. There are ten numbers each, or eighty in total, that reduce to a 1, 3, 4, 5, 6, 7, 8, or 9. There are nine numbers that reduce to an 11. There are two numbers that reduce to a 2. There is only one, or eight in total, which reduce to a 22, 33, 44, 55, 66, 77, 88, or a 99. That is eighty plus nine plus two plus eight, or ninety-nine in total."

"Interestingly, the master number 11 is almost as common as the single digits excluding the 2. That does not mean that it is a common number. This is not a random number generation. As a general matter you would not expect any master or power numbers from your average group of ninety-nine subjects."

"But given the uniqueness of this situation I would say every one of you all has already mastered and have unusual powers, but it may be temporary, so I say let us see, yes?"

"We will see what the Sphere has to say in the matter. She will be issuing the numbers for everyone other than "Ninety-Nine" and myself, we are already set. A thorough analysis would compute all sorts of numbers for each one of you, but we will just use this one at this time. Ninety-Nine and I will be down the hall and if you press the red button we will come running and if you just have a question press the green button and we will answer on the computer screen. Do not worry about waking us. We are here for you!"

"Uh Eighty-Eight, I am pressing the green button. But we cannot sleep, and our bodies are completely changed, and we are just so excited to learn what our numbers mean. Are you awake?"

"Yes. But first, who is this?" "This is Aristotle!"

"Ha-ha! Well, you sure hit the jackpot, yes? Aristotle was a great Greek philosopher and scientist. He was born just over 2,400 years ago and died 62 years later. He studied under Plato, and he taught widely upon the nature of the soul in both animate and inanimate bodies among other things. And Plato wrote about the five platonic solids during Aristotle's life. So, excellent! I take it you have a 38/11 on your sleep shirt."

"Yes, I do Ma'am. Yes, I do and everybody else has their numbers too. And we are all wide awake so if you might come down and talk to us it would help. Maybe we could go back to sleep after that. And everyone else has heard this conversation so you do not have to repeat it."

"How considerate of you. Thank you. I am on my way, Luvs! And I am bringing Ninety-Nine along with me. What a treat! We are so excited to see you all."

"And here we are my Luvs! Ha-ha! Is everyone wide awake?"
"Yeeeeeeeeessssss!"

"Awesome!"

"Well, let us start with you Aristotle, and we will work from there. Do you want to take this one or should I Ninety-Nine?"

"Carry on Eighty-Eight."

"Okay everyone, Aristotle has a 38/11 displayed upon his sleep shirt placed there by the Sphere herself. And this is most fortuitous. He also seems to have dreamed of his new name which has further empowered his awakening. We should all rejoice that he has presented himself to the colony in this manner and that he was the first to speak. Just wonderful!"

"Are there any others that have received a 38/11 upon their sleep shirts? If so, raise your hands and I will point to you one at a time and you may introduce yourself by your new name. Okay, you first, you second, and you third. Go! Ha-ha!"

"Timothy" "Joan" "Nikola"

"Holy cow! That would be Saint Timothy, Joan of Arc, and Nikola Tesla. That is a four-corner foundation of very powerful eleven energy for your group here but also for your colony to operate from. Even though we are remote they will also be receiving this energy just far less immediately and powerfully for now. We do not want to overwhelm them. And the four 11's combine for a forty-four energy also. But let's just look at the 38/11 for now."

"When interpreting numbers in numerology we read from the left to the right. So let us start with the 3. The 3 represents a wholeness on this planet. Like body-mind-soul or beginning-middle-end or start-do-stop. The 3 represents a creative-balanced-well-rounded energy. Very social and intellectual. That is, in part, because it includes the 1 and the 2 within it. The 1 is the initiator, the creator, and the singularity so to speak. It is irresistible and irrepressible. The 2 represents the confrontation with duality. It represents both the "is" and the "is not". So, getting from the 1 to the 3 is some work, yes? But the 2 also represents companionship and with your colony mind you will have no trouble with it."

"Moving on to the 8 it represents "as above so below." So, it represents harmonizing the heavens and the Earth plane. One must be high minded walking the path of the 8. The 8 has the 1 through the 7 in it. So, a very rich number. The 11 represents mastery of higher order knowledge and intuition. In terms of such knowledge and intuition it is the point of the spear, the singularity, the sensitive, and the rare visionary. We would say the 11 is the Master Thinker. Aristotle certainly was this and more."

"Now, we will speak briefly about Saint Timothy. Timothy means honoring or honored by God. He was born in 17 and died in 97. He was reserved and had a Jewish/Greek background. He traveled and taught with the Apostle Paul, and he is mentioned in the Catholic Bible and became a Bishop in the Church. At the age of 80, he was beaten and stoned to death by pagans and became a martyr. He was declared a Saint at that time."

"Now we speak briefly of Joan of Arc, who was born in 1412 and died in 1431. She was a French peasant girl who, at 13 years of age, began hearing the voices of Saint Margaret and Saint Catherine and the Archangel Michael. At 17 years of age, they told her to go to war to defeat the English army. And in just two years she did that. But she gave her life in the process. At 19 years of age, she was burned at the stake and subjected to other horrific assaults and character assassination. It took five hundred years before the Catholic Church canonized her as a Saint."

"Now we speak briefly about Nikola Tesla, born in 1856 and died in 1943. Mr. Tesla may have been the single most brilliant Earth Human Being ever. He was a prolific inventor, and he could speak eight languages and could read a book a single time and then repeat it verbatim without reference to the book. It is hard to even imagine that level of intellect. And he invented things that he hid and then others invented them. Surely evidence that he was a telepathic Higher Order Being in physical form."

"That is just a tremendous foundation Luvs! Nicely Done! Let's get some sleep now. Goodnight, All!"

"Wait, wait, wait. There is more that perhaps would be well stated at this time Eighty-Eight if I might speak."

"Carry on Ninety-Nine. Carry on." "Thank you Eighty-Eight."

"The 3 is also a symbol of the equilateral triangle. And the equilateral triangle is fundamental to three of the five platonic solids. The Tetrahedron, the Octahedron and the Icosahedron all so named for the number of faces they present."

"The Tetrahedron is constructed of four equilateral triangles, so it presents four faces. In this case they would represent the four of you. In sacred geometry the Tetrahedron represents Fire. Aside from the obvious physical reference, Fire in Human Beings represents extreme motivation for change of some sort. It also represents enlightenment and that spark of awareness so to speak. But above all else it represents spontaneous rapid change. As do the four of you in this regard."

"The Octahedron is constructed of eight equilateral triangles so there is your 3 and your 8 in the same form. In sacred geometry the Octahedron represents Air, the formless element of life on this planet. And the number 8 also represents "as above so below." But you will notice with the number 8 that the lines cross separating the above from the below. So as a symbol the number 8 is quite appropriate for a 3DC/4DC planet where harmonizing the heavens and the earth plane is arduous.

By way of contrast, the Octahedron as a harmonizing symbol is more appropriate for a 4DC/5DC planet. There is only a thin membrane separating the two dimensions of consciousness within the form. Not surprisingly, moving between them is routine on a 4DC/5DC planet. So, the eight faces in this case would represent the higher and lower selves of each of you."

"The Icosahedron is constructed of twenty equilateral triangles and in sacred geometry it represents water. Water, the seeming definition of elastic form, yes? Ha-ha! Anyhow, in the Icosahedron there are five faces for each of the four of you. One each for your Love Face, your Peace Face, your Harmony Face, your Tranquility Face, and your Unity Face. I am sure you four 11's, you four Master Thinkers will expand upon that considerably, but I just wanted to begin opening the conversation."

"Okay, thank you Ninety-Nine. That should certainly help most of us get a better night's sleep now. Ha-ha! Thank you, my Luv's, get yourself some more sleep now. Goodnight! Come on Ninety-Nine, step lightly. We do not want to wake them on the way out. Ha-ha!"

THE TRIP

"Wow, what a night my children! What a long night we all had and what a morning too. Let's all eat this hearty breakfast. This looks exactly like your favorite fish, but it has been manifested directly from the spirit. How about that, yes?"

"You all are surprisingly adept at the use of your new bodies. It was rigorous training, but you exceeded all expectations. We were outside of the linear timeline for two decades but this short mention of it is all that will be evidenced in the linear timeline even though, of course, it altered everything. You are just such a wonderful surprise for Ninety-Nine and me. For that matter for yourselves too! None would have thought we would have had such a huge success, but we did!"

"Anyhow, thank all of you for volunteering for this project. While from the perspective of Ninety-Nine and myself it is incapable of any error of any sort it may seem less perfect than that from your perspective. We only say that to pop that little resistance balloon. Of course, you would feel that the first time you travel in intergalactic space. Many of you all also hesitated when we said forty-four. And that would be because you thought of yourselves as bodies and not as spirits. And as spirits I am sure you can feel the oneness with your mates is different than being just bodies. However, acknowledging that is not enough for intergalactic travel. No, it requires that every one of us is one with every other one of us. So that we become only one. To travel at such profound speeds and distances we must achieve Unity and to achieve Unity we must first achieve, in order, Love, Peace, Harmony and Tranquility."

"Starting with Love. Love is woven into the fabric which holds the Universe together. So, our transit will only be as successful as our ability to Love not just each other but the entire Universe, and that is why we must Love each other so much that we are one with each other. Any failure to Love each other as one represents a twig that may catch on the fabric and do us harm. So, chant with me if you would. I am one. I am one. I am one. Notice how there are 99 variations of that chant. You can hear each one of us in the chant. Let us continue."

"I am one. I am one. I am one.... I AM! AND WE ARE! ONE! I AM! AND WE ARE! LOVE! Oh My God, this is exquisite. I am just soaring and expanding out into the Universe all around me. So, I need to be at Peace because I am just so intrusive, I am banging off the walls. But I Love banging off the walls. I just Love the sensation of the physicality of Love. But being Peace is being entirely devoid of any conflict or disturbance at all. So, I will focus on the Love of being present to the wonder of all that is around me without disturbing it. For that is the essence of Peace. It is the Love of being present to the wonder of all that is around me without disturbing it. But I notice that I am still banging into the walls so to speak. That is because there is a rhythm to the Universe, and we need to mimic it. We cannot go in a straight line if the energy vectors in the Universe are rhythmic, but we also do not want to travel right down the center of the freeway, so to speak. We can uniquely harmonize with the energy vectors and slipstream effortlessly beside them and through all of this and more we achieve tranquility. It is as if we are truly motionless. As if we are just absorbing the deep wisdom continuously available to us during our passage."

"WE ARE! AND I AM! LOVE! WE ARE! AND I AM! PEACE! WE ARE! AND I AM! HARMONY! WE ARE! AND I AM! TRANQUILITY! WE ARE! AND I AM! UNITY!"

"Okay, how does everybody feel? Yeah, you cannot speak yet, yes? Ha-ha! Take your time. It seemed like just a short conversation, but we covered quite a bit of turf. Ha-ha! Please drink some water. There is a bottle for each of you and I would not try to talk or walk or even stand up until after you have consumed the whole bottle. Pass them around. We are going to rest for a bit as you all begin to become more active. Please do not stir us until all of you are fully awake and standing and walking about. Thanks!"

"Wow! I am whooped! Ha-ha! How about you Ruby?"

"I am completely with you on that, Earnest! One hundred percent! I just do not think I have ever been this tired. If they can take a nap then so can we and I am taking a nap NOW! Ha-ha!"

"Well Ruby, it looks unanimous to me so let's head on back to our wonderful Sphere sleep room. I am so happy that she put a 22 on my sleep shirt and a 33 on your sleep shirt. That makes me a Master Builder and you a Master Teacher. So cool."

"Okay everybody! I think that as soon as half of us are up and about then they should get the rest of us up. Otherwise, I say let the others sleep. Everybody in? Okay, then it is a deal."

"Take my hand and let's go Ruby!"

"Hey sleepyheads, this is your captain, the amazing Ninety-Nine himself speaking. Ha-ha! Let's wake up and get out of this joint, yes? We need to be stretching our legs and we do not want to go alone so you all wake up now."

"Okay, okay, okay! We are all up and about, but we are still tired and sore. I can understand the tired but what is the sore all about? Where did that come from?"

"We are not precisely sure, Ruby, but as they say, Intergalactic travel is not for sissies. The first time we did it we were sick for a month. It just got our insides all messed up."

"Yeah, Boss, but we were just training so does the training do that to you too? I mean I am glad to know that because it would have made me fearful if I was on a trip."

"You all pop that main door open and let's get on out of here now. I am sure the fresh air will clear our heads and strengthen our legs."

"What the Heck is that Boss? It looks like everything is sort of shaded in light white and blue. And it is very still. Is it a blue moon or something?"

"Earnest, that is the Fifth Dimensional half of our home planet. We are now on the other side of the Universe on our planet, and it is a 4DC/5DC planet. And being a 4DC/5DC planet it is complex. The 5DC half is form for the most part. It has substance, but not much compared to the 4DC half. It is an anomaly we have learned to Love. The planet moves and rotates like it is perfectly balanced which it is not. But it acts exactly like it is and so it is, yes? The 5DC half allows us to easily travel all over the Universe at will. So, it is convenient. We can just dock here and hop out the door and fly and/or float down to the 4DC part. We have done it a thousand times and we have never been hurt."

"Yeah, Boss, but we are Penguins and we only met you a bit ago and we have never even talked before you tweaked our brains, and now, we are on the other side of the Universe. Our women are too stunned to even breath right now but as soon as they get their breath there is going to be a weeping and wailing and gnashing of beaks like has never been heard before. I cannot believe you took us all the way to the other side of the Universe without allowing us to say we did not want to go. I mean we were just being nice to you."

"Now, now, now, Earnest, you and your Love, Ruby, are the reason we are all here. So, we do not see how you all have much to complain about. And we have known each other for decades now. Maybe not in linear time but in real time."

"Well Boss, it is clear to me that you do not know 3DC/4DC women, or you would know that saying they do not have much to complain about is a losing argument."

"Earnest, Earnest, Love, would you please shut that door while we compose ourselves. Thank you! Boss, I do not think you realize that Earnest is underselling the upset. Boss, please tell us this is all just some sort of illusion that you made up to test us and we will gladly admit that we failed the test and we do not want to go."

"Ruby, Ruby, Love, we would do that if we could do that, but it would not be true. We are on our planet on the other side of the Universe from your planet."

"But Boss, everybody must be worried sick about us right about now. I mean we did not tell anyone goodbye or anything. And we are a Colony, everyone knows everyone. It is not right."

"We took care of that Ruby. We sort of cloned you all, so nobody even knows you are gone. By the time we get back you might want to start over as a Human Being or something. Or you might just want to stay right here. This is a fine planet, and it has many benefits compared to your planet. Once you have seen some of those you may feel differently."

"You made doubles of us, Boss? So, there is a Ruby and an Earnest back on our Mother Earth, and no one can tell the difference? And what happens when we go back? I mean, will not "that Ruby and Earnest" have experiences with the Colony that they will remember, and we will not even know about? How are we to get our lives back? And isn't that the same for every one of us, Boss? One day we are there and then our double is there and nobody notices the change and then maybe we can't go back. Yikes! I mean, if we did go back would our double have to die or something? That would be sad. That would be just like we were dying in a way would it not, Boss?"

"Guys, guys, guys! We appreciate your inquiries and efforts to understand the ramifications of your travel to our planet. But just consider your double the remote you or vice versa."

"Okay, help me out Ruby. Is Boss telling us that we might be the doubles? He may think that should comfort us, but does that mean we are not real?"

"Earnest, I think this is what Boss means when he says he is above the fighter pilots pay grade. We are not going to be able to understand this now and I am simply fine with that."

"Ruby, let us say one more thing. When we go back, we will go back to the moment just before the, let us use the word, remotes were created. We are not in linear time anymore."

"Well, Boss, I am taking comfort from not being in linear time anymore. Before we met you, I would have been terrified of the concept but now I have a death grip on it. Thanks!"

"What does everyone want to do? Shall we rest for the evening and then go down in the morning? If we get up early enough, we can see the over/under sunrise. Is anyone beginning to get hungry or thirsty? Yes? Okay Let's do a meditation. Picture yourself drawing in your breath from the entire extension of the 5DC aspect of our planet. Good, and now use your body to breath as a single organ, not through your lungs but through every atom and molecule of your body. Now, think of what is missing and inhale that and repeat this form of breathing over and over until you are filled to overflowing. Whatever 5DC seems to lack in space and time is more than made up for by the feasts for immortals, yes?"

"Our people are all a buzz. They would like to have you come to 4DC and let them show you some of the sights. Even tonight we could go out and look at the over/under moons. Our people can see both moons and they can see the thin boundary between the 4DC and 5DC, but few seem willing to cross it very often. We are an anomaly in that regard. Our 4DC is spectacular and our people are not very motivated to experience more than that. There are no wars, no hunger, no poverty, no sickness. You name a negative and it is not here."

"In the case of your planet which is 3DC/4DC the movement is bottom up so the 4DC is the positive of the 3DC without the negative. In the case of our planet which is 4DC/5DC the movement is top down so the 4DC is the positive of 5DC without the extraordinary space and time mastery. So, the two 4DC's are quite different."

"Our people have considered us sort of eclectic, but our status went up considerably when your planet got into trouble. It started with the wars and pandemics of your 20th century, and it has continued into your 21st century but not with the extreme harshness of your 20th century. It was not you're doing but you may have noticed it although we did not. That is, not until we came to your planet to check on your local 5DC traveler and we found out about all the rest, and we have been at work with your planet ever since."

"As we have said, it seemed that your Sun was about to launch a coronal mass extrusion which would strike the Earth and kill everything one thousand miles deep into the planet. At least that is what our best scientists saw as a future for your Earth. It appears that the demise for your Earth has been diminished now but there are others upon the way. None of them will be good for you and some will also be bad for us and other sentient beings in the Universe. So, our people dispatched us to help those trying to fix the problem. They told us if we found anything particularly interesting, we should bring it back to them and they are incredibly happy that we have brought you and your people's music back to them."

"The combinations of the notes and the lyrics in the music are just pure genius. Our music has nothing comparable. I suppose there is something to be said for 3DC/4DC, yes? Ha-ha! As for you Penguins, well we had never even conceived of such a life form and when we found that you all exhibited such love and light, we just had to bring you back to meet our people. We will see you all first thing in the morning. Wake whenever you want but we will rise from our rest when it is time to get ready to go."

TESTED ON 4DC

"It is a bit before our 4DC sunrise which the 5DC aspect of our planet mimics just like with our moon. So, we will have the magnificent sight of an over/under sunrise. We will, that is, if all the sleepy heads will get up, please. I mean it would be bad form to have to be alarmed out of your bed like you do on your planet. I completely understand. But let's step lively now out onto the main deck. Eighty-Eight how about helping that side wake up and I will work this side."

"Will do, Boss! I have been waiting for the opportunity to call you that. I have always said you are kind of Bossy, yes? Come on now my little Penguin children let's wake up!"

"Okay, the eleven of us from ninety through Ninety-Nine plus my Eighty-Eight are all at the front door ready to go. Couples one through forty-four will line up sequentially and we will head out the front door. Hold onto the rails as you come out. There is little gravity in the 5DC half of the planet but there is some and so, we will be tethered to each other with a rope."

"Eighty-Eight will be the last one out and I will be first. Pop your wings out and let's fly on down, yes? Pretty amazing, we are eleven miles above the 4DC/5DC membrane, and we are flying. Everybody doing okay back there. This is your first flight but Eighty-Eight and I are your fail safe, yes? How could we let you miss this beautiful over/under sunrise? I mean really! And in addition to the minimal gravity, you are also very buoyant now. So, when we get to the 4DC we can return to our 5DC Sphere very easily. Or if you all would like to stay in 4DC tonight then I will call the Sphere, and we can stay in it in 4DC. How does that sound? Silence, eh? What is going on back there, Eighty-Eight?"

"I would say pure terror Boss. Pure terror, but nobody is getting hurt."

"Are we going to be able to set them down gently if they are unconscious, Eighty-Eight?"

"What about me Boss? What if I am unconscious? I mean when I heard you say eleven, I was expecting the next word to be feet or yards but I almost fainted when I heard you say miles."

"Eighty-Eight you are doing great! You are the strongest woman I have ever met, and you are not going to lose consciousness. You are just messing with me. I can respect that! Nicely Done!"

"Yeah, whatever you say Boss! Except, I am eleven miles above the ground Boss and my heart is beating mighty fast. I did not expect them to all pass out but eleven miles Boss!! Whew!"

"That is good Eighty-Eight! Just play with it and have some fun with it. Make a song out of it or make a game out of it. Just keep working on it and it will all be fine. It looks like we only have one more mile to go and we got to slow this thing down right now. So, meet me at the top and let's pull it up to a stop. Nicely done, Eighty-Eight!! Nicely done!"

"Okay, now let's lower it slowly and we can set two down at a time from the middle. If they cannot stand up, we can just gently tilt them until they are laying on the ground. What a trip!"

"Maybe you are right that probably was a bit much for the first time flying. But my goodness, they are just such troopers and such sweethearts I forget that they are complete novices. If there is any net harm to them, we will just go back in time and redo it. Let's sit them all up in a circle as if we have been meditating for a bit and then we will wake them."

"Okay everybody, how did you like your first free fall flight? You did just fantastic. You are calm and unhurt and that was the highest jump novices have ever done. We are so proud of you!!"

"Boss, I have got to admit. Just when I think you have done all the terrorizing of us that you could possibly do you go and bring out another event for us to survive. Are you done yet?"

"Yes Earnest, this is the end game that we are in now. We came here for this. A planet with tremendous beauty like that which was your Mother Earth's intended legacy until it was spoiled. There are no manufactured forms of travel here. The species of Human Being here remote views or travels by Merkabah or flies with the wings we have and which you now have also. We are whole numbers dimensionally. We are either nine, ten or eleven feet tall and you all are either three, four, or five feet tall and our wings are twice our heights. There are no predators on the planet. Everything here is fueled by the fabric of the Universe. So, no one and no thing is particularly susceptible to forced labor of one form or another and we have no need to abuse our planet to house and transport ourselves. And we have no need to form into groups for massive projects either. This is as much of a free will choice planet as one can imagine. There is tremendous natural beauty and our planet changes for us all by herself to keep the allure so to speak."

"You will fit right in with your songs and your invented ability to speak and move as a single organism. That will be endlessly fascinating for my people. How did you do that anyway?"

"We are not saying Boss. We do not want you all to get bored with us exactly right away anyhow. Truth be known we are not sure how we did it anyhow. Seemed more like it just happened."

"Fair enough, Earnest. Let's go practice some low altitude flying as we process ourselves onto the planet. The atmosphere restricts to whom it will grant entrance. You passed! But the planet continually monitors the activities of visitors to the planet. So, until you are asked to make this your home and accept that request you should know you are being monitored."

"There is a nice landscape just beyond that tree line in the distance. Let's fly in that direction and find a route in the trees that will take us to breathtaking beauty. It is a few miles distant, and we can spend as much time feeling out our wings a few feet above this flat ground as you would prefer. Earnest and Ruby, please lead us in that direction."

"Boss, before we get to the tree line can we soar a little bit. I think I have the hang of it now and Ruby is asking me in my mind, so to speak, to ask you out loud. So, she is good to go also!"

"As much as you would like my friend. As much as you would like. If we get to an altitude where we can see the landscape, then perhaps we will just fly directly there. Again, your choice."

"Oh My God! I see what you mean Boss! There is a massive canyon up ahead with just magnificent colors in it. They seem to be moving. What is that Boss?"

"We will see when we get there, Earnest! We will see! The canyon responds to whomever it is interacting with. And it is displaying resplendent beauty for you two. Nicely Done!! Let's go down one of the little rivulets running into the canyon and look for a contained area with a pond. We will practice a bit before venturing into the main canyon."

"This area looks delightful Earnest. Let's set down in it and see what sort of practice we will be needing. I am thinking it will be a bit more arduous than we might expect."

"Ha-ha!! So, you are a psychic now, eh Ruby? Ha-ha!! Yeah, it will probably be a bit more arduous than you expect. But like everything else it will enrich you immensely. When you and

Earnest have completed this training, you will be ecstatic and happier than you can ever remember. Once the light turns on in you it will be impeccable, logical, and intuitive. So far, the canyon has suppressed itself and really responded to you very gently. And it will not seek to just suddenly startle you now. But you may find some of the training to be startling. We call this canyon JAG Canyon. That is short for Joy and Gratitude. When you are expressing Joy and Gratitude you are winning, and the canyon returns it to you, and you move up. If you are expressing wealthier than the canyon baths you in poorer than. If you are expressing better than the canyon baths you in worse than. For smarter than you get dumber than."

"A note of caution. If you express, you can't do this or that to me the canyon will erupt in laughter. Better to just skip that thought unless you enjoy being embarrassed. Anyhow, you will each head down your separate side of the canyon. I will follow above you just monitoring the colors to determine your progress. When it all goes white you win!!"

"You will be inside the colors, and you will be confronted with challenges as you move down the canyon. There may be beasts. But mostly they will be ordinary challenges in your life. Nothing can harm you when you are in the white light. And almost nothing can help you in the absence of light. Fortunately, you will start your journey in the brightest of bright white light. But you will not remember this conversation and it may all seem like a bad dream at best and like a terrible reality at worst. I will leave advice in the form of notes upon your path."

"The training is hard but rarely fatal. This would be considered a funny comical stroll down the canyon for a Master of the Light. But it can get out of control and spiral into darkness also. As a matter of fact, it can spiral out of control for a Master of the Light also. But they have sophisticated recovery mechanisms, so they get back into the white light quickly."

"When we have all gotten through our paces and tests, we will meet and either discuss abstractly or share intimate details of the nature of our respective passages. Are there any questions? Okay then, those with odd numbers, head into the side of the canyon to my left and those with even numbers, head into the side of the canyon to my right. Good! Each of your passages will be unique to you. When the person ahead of you disappears from your sight then you need to follow to that same entry point and commence your passage."

"What about me Boss? I am number Eighty-Eight. Do I go with the even numbers, or do I even go? And are you going? I mean you have done this before right?"

"Yes, Eighty-Eight and those are good questions. You will enter on the side of the Canyon to my right, and you will follow number Eighty-Six and so you will rotate through the entire program with our lovely Penguins. It will be wonderful, yes?"

"In the interim, I will fly up and down the canyon looking for any colors that are of concern and I will help liberate any of our crew that gets stuck so that they are not stuck for long. Okay then! How is everybody doing? That was an eye opener, yes? Ha-ha! And people unfamiliar with the extraordinary intention required to ascend refer to this as Lala Land!! Is there even one of you, after having just has gone through the planets testing of you in order that you might be allowed to dwell here, who would use the term Lala Land?"

"Where are Lady Master and Master First-In and Last-Out? Yeah, there they are! They demanded to be number one and two so that they were the first in and then we had to bring them out. They could not even bring themselves out! Raise your hands if you saw either of them when you were in there? Yeah, everybody! How many were too fearful to stop and render aid? Yeah, everybody!"

"They are no bigger than a minute and just beautiful young Penguins. Maybe they did not have sufficient strength. Maybe they did not have sufficient toughness. Or maybe we just never understood them. Or maybe we just never understood the test. Did anyone see anyone else while you were in there? Raise your hand if you did. No hands up? So, you all are saying that either she or he is the only one of us you saw while inside the canyon. Wonder what that means? Any ideas? Ha-ha! Yeah, you are going to love this!"

"Well, they volunteered to help everyone else upon their transit by taking some of their emotional baggage from them. The fear that you felt when you saw them was that fear leaving you. Of course, the fear that left you was absorbed by them, and it eventually killed them. But not before the rest of us excluding myself and "Eighty-Eight" had off loaded fears to them."

"You are bigger, and some outweigh them two to one. So, you can imagine how much of your fear they had to carry. They are tough but you overwhelmed hem, and they died. But nobody dies on our watch! So, we are going to bring them back and they will be our Ninety-Seven and Ninety-Eight now and everyone will move up and we will repeat the process. You will have your memories delayed until we have completed this process for every one of you. And that will take forty-nine iterations for us to process the ninety-seven of you plus my Eighty-Eight, two at a time."

"Each additional time we go through this you will not consciously remember that you had ever done it before. It is a rigorous process. And "Eighty-Eight" is joining to balance you. Initially, when the memories are released, many will get very nauseated with predictable results. But that changes as the memories continue to flood the collective consciousness. It changes to chuckles and eventually to hysterical laughter. And we are all free of our personal and collective fears. It works every time. It starts as a nightmare and ends as a great comedy! But you must live it. It is the living of it that penetrates so deep into your consciousness that you are freed. So, we do not typically mention it until we are knee deep in it. Questions?"

"No questions. Okay then, lay down where you are and go to sleep and we will start over again when we wake up. We will bring the little ones back and you will all have delayed memory, and we will start over in the new order thinking it is the first time for us to do it. We will begin accelerating as we go through it until all 98 of you have been through the process. Then we will sit in a circle having this discussion for the last time and we will release the memories and we will all hold onto our socks, yes? Yes! It will rock all of us, but no one will die and we will be fearless and laughing hysterically as we complete the process and we may need a week or more to recover from our efforts on this day in Lala Land, yes? Yes! Ha-ha!"

THE SHOW

"Just a magnificent performance my little ones! Just magnificent! You earned the highest honors from the JAG. Pure White Light within you and all around you! Thank you! It has taken quite a while for us to recover. We have been sleeping for several weeks integrating the profound transitions we have initiated in our lives. Again, thank you! Now we have a show to put on. So, let's get ready. Everybody, up and doing your stretches now and let's breathe in a full complement of energy from the Universe. Yes! Head on over to the gymnasium for muscular exercise, the stage for artistic dance and colony forms practice and the music room for singing practice. Limber up those vocal cords. Eighty-Eight and I will be moving around to help as we see a need but if you have questions just holler out and we will come to you.

Okay, are we ready to go now? Is everybody ready for and excited about our next initiative?"

"Yeeeeeeeeeeeeeeeeeeeeessssssssssssssssssssss!!!!!

"Great! Where is Eighty-Eight? Come on girl, we start the show singing and dancing. Everybody else get ready and watch us. Watch for our signal's performers, and stage managers get ready to feed the acts onto the stage. You all are the ones that we need to support us in a seamless show. This is the first Intergalactic show of its kind. We are perfect. We were made for this moment. We would not want to be anywhere else in the Universe at this time. The Sphere is filling up with our fellow Star Planet citizens and the excitement is just electric. We have never come back from a trip with such wonderful things to share with them. Never!!

Please go backstage now and get your costumes on and we will get you lined up and organized to participate in the show. It will be so much fun you will love it! Now on to the Party, yes?"

"Greetings and Salutations my Beautiful, Blessed and Beloved citizens of this phenomenal Star Planet of ours. I am Ninety-Nine and along with my beloved Eight-Eight we are the Masters of Ceremonies this evening. She is just so beautiful! Please give her a hand!"

I bow and the crowd cheers and roars forever it seems. And I calm them down and they settle back into their seats.

"It has been a hard trip but so, so, so rewarding! And we could not have done it without Mission Control and his team of devoted wizards keeping track of us! Please stand-up ladies and gentlemen. Let's give them a hand now!" And the crowd is back on its feet cheering and roaring and clapping and stomping their feet! The energy level is going through the roof!

"We are exceedingly proud to present to you direct from Planet Earth on the other side of the Universe a Parade of Precious Penguins! Bring it ladies!"

The band starts pounding it out to up the level of excitement and on cue out onto the stage strutting come Paula, Priscilla and Penelope dressed in Black and White sequined dresses singing a song!

There are dozens and dozens of other penguins creating the scene all around them. Just wonderful They are so cocky! They are not backing down! Ha-ha! The crowd is on its feet, and I do not see them sitting down for quite a while. Oops, they drag Eighty-Eight and me out onto the stage with them and we are caught up in the music and dancing our lights out! Great they have us center stage cameoing us. The crowd is loving it. They are laughing their heads off. So are we for that matter!

"Okay then! How about that, yes? Indeed! Just wonderful! Next, we are going to do what we call a colony song. That is, a group of the colony is going to shape shift into a single being and one or more of us will sing a song to you as they give you an artistic expression of the emotional interior of the singer songwriter."

There is a lot of sorrow and hardship on Planet Earth. This is a song about change and songs like these are about as authentic as you can get. Hit it! "The band begins prelude music as dozens of our Precious Penguins band together center stage and become one and then a twenty-two-foot-tall being, representing an artistic expression of the emotional interior of the singer songwriter that wrote the song they are singing, is looking at the audience and with no idea how they will understand sets out to convey the message of the song to them with enormous heart."

There is not another sound in the Sphere! Rapt Attention! I think if anyone made a sound, they would all start crying! And I stand when our Penguins are done, and they run off stage. But I call them back to center stage to be with me. I say to the audience, "These are wisdom songs my friends. It is alright to celebrate the wisdom being conveyed even if you would dread being engulfed by it. So, how about if we get out of our seats and give these tiny warriors with enormous hearts a big hand, yes? That was not an easy song for them!"

That breaks it. The tears are flowing everywhere but everyone is on their feet and clapping and cheering and breathing. They had stopped breathing. Ha-ha!

"Okay, okay! Shake it off! Yeah, that's good! I love all these songs but most of them will not be a day at the beach or a walk in the park as the Earth Human Beings say. We have another song about changing for you and then we will have some interpretative comments to deliver to you. And then we will have a final song which may have you laughing a bit. Overall, I believe at the end of the evening you will be very grateful that you came. So, are you revitalized? Are you ready to roar?"

Yeeeeesssss!

"I can't hear you!"

Yeeeeeeeeeessssssssss!!

"Nope, I still can't hear you!"

Yeeeeeeeeeeeeeeeeeeeeessssssssssssssssssssss!!!!

"Alright then!" And our Precious Penguins shape-shift into another twenty-two-foot-tall being and start singing and we are off to the races. Once again, Rapt Attention as we sing another song with changing at its heart. Our audience just said to heck with it and started crying and cheering at the same time. They are whistling and hooting, and they are stomping their feet because they want these Precious Penguins to stay with us and illuminate some things and become a part of us. You can feel it, it is thick in the Sphere.

"WOW! Thank you, my people! Thank You! My stage manager and his team are bringing out some things for us to sit on so we can have a conversation with you now. Eighty-Eight and I will sit in the middle, each in an overstuffed chair and we will have two long couches angled forward from contact with our chairs for our Precious Penguins to sit on."

"At some time in our conversation, you will be able to ask them a few questions. But not too many, they are tired, but they will not stop unless told to stand down. They will die first. We will not let that happen! They are in the back composing themselves. We have asked them to present themselves in their pre-contact form. We have not done that since we first upgraded them. They are a little concerned about it. Ha-ha! Come out when you are ready my Luvs!"

Then out they come, ninety-seven little one-or-two-foot-tall Fairy Penguins waddling to the couches and hopping up on them. No legs, no arms, no hands, no wings. Just Fairy Penguins.

"Okay, then. This is their starting point from maybe a year ago in linear time. They were completely owned by space and time then. I mean, the species of Human Beings upon their planet are completely owned by space and time and so how could this diminutive species not be similarly owned. The dominant species always sets the tone for every other species upon a planet. Under our guiding hand they have managed to escape space and time completely and they will flourish upon this planet, yes?"

"Absolutely! Bravo! Bravo! Bravo! You Precious Penguins you! Bravo! Eighty-Eight and Ninety-Nine, can you send them back and let them recompose themselves to who they are now and then return to us?"

"Indeed, we can Mission Control! And we will if that would be their desire! Ha-ha! Well, I guess the empty couches tell us all we need to know about that. We can carry on in their absence. They will return when they are comfortable doing so."

"Okay, who wants to carry on a conversation with me? Yikes, quite a few. But as is our way that will sort out to only one or two in a moment. Perfect, and you two are?"

"I am Thirty-Three and she is Sixty-Six. Of course, we have so called given names, but they compute to these numbers. And we add to a Ninety-Nine, so we are your match, yes? Ha-ha!"

"I am sure you will be up to the task! Please ask your first question Thirty-Three." "Have you given full consideration to the potential dangers of bringing these beings into our midst?"

"Yes, next question. I believe you are up Sixty-Six."

"Thank you, sir! Have you had any disciplinary problems or medical problems or any casualties with your Penguins?"

"No, next question. I believe you are up Thirty-Three." "Okay, why did you have them perform the two sad songs?"

"I would not refer to them as sad songs. I would refer to them as trapped consciousness songs. I would refer to them as songs of impotence or songs of powerlessness. You are not familiar with this kind of song because you are a Fifth Dimensional Consciousness, a 5DC. The only saving grace for the singers of these songs is that something larger than their entrapment is going to change life for the better for them. At many levels they are so, so, so, right about that but not at the level of the 5DC."

"It is easy to be 5DC on this planet because that consciousness is being cocreated by everyone on the planet and by the planet itself. When you visit a 3DC planet it taxes every ounce of your 5DC to remain 5DC. Eighty-Eight and I did it, but we had Mission Control monitoring us to true us up from time to time."

"Let me interject. I only had one time to use the phrase "truing up" with these two and it was ultimately an embarrassment to me that I used it. In hindsight, I felt I had simply overreacted."

"Thank you, Mission Control!"

"Anyhow, the history of the species of Human Beings upon Mother Earth is one in which the strong have ruthlessly exploited the weak everything. Not just the weaker 99% of the Human Species but the Planet herself and everything else upon her. Ha-

ha! You cannot make this stuff up! Ha-ha! And, drum roll please, our planet has adopted Mother Earth."

"Thank you for the cymbals, Earnest!"

"The adoption has its own possible and potential poor outcomes for us, but perhaps we can best move toward addressing them by first addressing the issues with the newly 5DC Penguins on our planet right now, yes? The Penguins might give us a vital understanding that allows us to extract ourselves from the many predicaments in which the Mother Earth planet has placed us. But we shall see, yes?"

"Dimensions of lesser consciousness have described the 5DC as being outside of space and time. And that is likely because from their perspective we seemingly pop in and out of space and time at will. And since we have all come from lesser levels of consciousness, we have probably continued to use that phrase from prior personal levels. But it is incorrect. We are not outside of space and time. There is space and time here right now, yes?"

"The truth is that we have dominion over space and time. We are senior to space and time, and we can leave it or enter it before or after the point of our exit. And when we do that, we simply become formless in the fields of all possibility and potentiality to exit and we reenter into form in some other space and time. And so long as we remain formless, we can travel anywhere in the Universe at the speed of thought."

"Our Penguins do not have that capacity yet, so they are modified 5DC. We have told them it is temporary subject to it all working out so to speak. But we fully anticipate that it will become permanent. And we have taken them through JAG Canyon, and they achieved a Pure White Light exit."

"That's right, Pure White, give them a big, big hand! Thank you! Any more questions? No? Okay!"

"We have one more song for you. It is a song that is quite revealing when sung by our Mother Earth. Our Star Planet has adopted Mother Earth, and it is above my pay grade to stand in judgement of that decision. I assume the decision is consistent with her impeccable history of wise decisions. And I have no information to think otherwise."

"The song is about being addicted and not wanting to break the habit and Mother Earth is addicted to her species of Human Beings. So, our Penguins will perform it as a colony song with Mother Earth singing it. Hit it!"

The band begins playing some prelude music and the colony pours onto the stage and joins into one. When they flesh out their form, they are in the form of Mother Earth. Her body and head are united as a round globe. But she has long arms and legs and fancy shoes on her feet. She is twenty- two feet tall, and her legs are eleven feet tall. And she has red on her cheeks, bright red lipstick on her lips, black mascara on her ultra large eyelashes and long flowing black hair. She is just crawling with billions and billions and billions of beings all over her just biting her everywhere. And she is coughing, and smells are emanating from her and there are dark clouds of noxious fumes all around her. All of which she pretends not to notice even as she is constantly itching herself somewhere or another with each of her hands. And she clears her throat as she tries to compose herself and then she begins belting out her song with power and velocity.

"How about that my people? Let's give our Precious Penguins a large round of applause. Great! And they are insisting that I not make them end on such heavy energy and so one more song before we go, yes? yes!"

And the band begins playing some prelude music and our Penguins come out floating in a gondola beneath a Balloon. And they are singing their hearts out in a song expressing Happiness. And they float out into the large Sphere over the crowd, and they are dropping stuffed baby Penguin dolls everywhere as they sing beautifully. And handfuls of them launch themselves out of the gondola as they sing. They fully extend their wings and soar around the room, and some go back to the inner Sphere, but most go down to say hi to the crowd in person. They have such a keen awareness of disturbances in the colony, so to speak, and of how to heal them. Excellent!

"Ha-ha! My people! Our Penguins are a perfect fit for us. Notice what they did there. They had a keen awareness of the disturbance I was creating in your joyful nature, and they took the initiative and fixed it! Let's give them a big hand! And you Precious Penguins take your bows! Ha-ha! Good night, all!"

And with that we leave the stage.

"Oh My God, you guys were fantastic! I told you they would love you. Nothing to fear but fear itself, yes? Let's get cleaned up and get some rest if needed and wanted. Doing the show in the 5DC was enormously draining.

There is no gravity of note in the 5DC and so it took skill and a lot more energy than upon your Mother Earth to perform our acts. We bow before your magnificence. We have never heard you sing so crisply and dance with such precision and enter and exit the stage with such perfection. Let's go sit around and share our experiences. I will shut up. This is your time so make the most of it my Luvs!"

"Wow, they disappeared at the speed of thought Eighty-Eight."

"Yes, they did, and we will let them have all the time they want and need. This was big!"

ASCENSION

"Okay everybody, wake up now and breathe in the delicious white light all around us. We are in the ascended ranges of the planet and so by definition we are ascended. Nicely done! Nicely done my sweet babies!! You are the first Penguins in the Universe to have done this. Ninety-Nine and I are so proud of you we could just burst!"

"I am especially proud of you because I personally traveled down the entire forty-nine paths of the JAG upon which you traveled, and it was not an easy passage even for me. Ninety-Nine just could not stop talking about how proud he is of your performances and especially your ad-lib song."

"Just magnificent!! You have ascended from the Earth before the Human Beings upon the planet have ascended. You are heavy lifting Penguins! Meant in the best of ways, yes? Ha-ha! More importantly you are permanent 5DC now. Congratulations! Give yourselves a big hand."

"Of course, you are thinking about going back to bring the rest of the Colony to this planet with you. Now is the time to do so before you get to love it here and will not leave. So, let's just chill a bit now in our Sphere and when we awaken, we will be upon your planet Earth just behind your Colony. It will be night so they will not notice our arrival. We will be in the exact same location from which we left, and it is only a few hours after our departure. The duplicates have not been fully activated yet and, on this timeline, they will not be. So, let's get some sleep my lovelies and prepare ourselves to enroll in your Colony for the trip to your new planet. We will enroll them with our love and our feats of daring do, yes? Ha-ha!"

"I will sleep here with you all and Ninety-Nine will take us to your Planet Earth. We will just play it by ear when we get there. You are familiar with the issues that might arise and can head them off at the pass so to speak. Good night, all!"

"Good night, Miss Boss! We are just glad to have crossed paths with you and your lovely man Ninety-Nine. In short, Master Love and I and all our dear friends that are with us now must be the luckiest penguins in the Universe! And I mean, really!! But we are tired and so just wake us when we get there. Ha-ha!!"

"Someone get the door; I hear a knocking on it. We must have awakened someone. Any ideas who it might be? Are there any notorious poor sleepers among your Colony? Ha-ha!"

"Oh My God! It is Sweet Pea! You come in here girl! What are you doing up at this hour? Why are you not with your mom and dad and all the others? And how is it that we are talking?"

"I was watching and listening when the man gave you his mind and his language Gram Ruby. And I got some of it too. And I have been telling all my friends and we thought we had lost you! We cried and went up and down the beach for hours trying to find you and then I saw the Sphere. I had looked here before and not seen it but there it was and so I knocked. My friends are outside. They are hiding because they are scared but we all know this is important and so we have looked for you and we have found you even though we were terrified. Please do not leave us like that again. We were so, so sad, and so, so scared. They got the man's mind and language from me, and we felt lonely without adults to think with and talk too."

"Well, let's go get your mother's up and see what we can do. If they find you with us this late at night, they will be mighty angry. They will not understand, and their understanding is needed. Anyhow, let's go, all of you get in the middle and we will walk you back to the Colony. Who is your friend Sweet Pea? He seems to stay close to you. And he is always smiling. No fear there!"

"He is known as Pushup and Cherub! Surprisingly, he was born with wings. And a smiling baby boy with wings. Cherub seems about right for him! But his birth name is different than that."

"We will call him Pushup. He is very strong and so is his dad, and we will need him to mature quickly. And you will need to mature quickly, also young lady. And you are doing spectacularly, yes?"

"Ha-ha! Well, I hope so Gram Ruby! Things could have gone poorly if we had not found you. And I was the one that got everybody out here hunting for you with me."

"Look up there. There is the Colony and Penguins are starting to stir. Quickly, go find your parents and give them hugs. And, if they are upset with you be nice and they will quickly get over it."

We go through the mind enhancements with the entire colony. It is a bit disturbing to them at first just as it was for us, but they adapt quicker than we did. It is the colony mind we have. When one or more of us has experienced something, it quickly becomes part of the colony mind and memory. Anyhow, that done, we quickly moved on.

"Good morning, everyone. We have a beautiful day before us. And I know that everyone is hungry but before going into the water today I want you to look at this picture screen. It is no secret that there are more than 1,000 of us heading into the water for breakfast. This picture screen shows that there are Leopard Seals here and Killer Whales there. Over here are other water dangers and here are the dangers from above. They are all waiting for us to head into the water to eat breakfast. But before we do so today, we are going to improve our odds of survival. We got upgraded inside the Sphere. Uh-huh!"

"We are bigger, faster, and smarter and we are now frightening our enemies. So, we are going to start by disrupting the water terrorists plans first. Watch as we go after the seals and whales. Uno and Duo are leading flights attacking the birds. We are bigger and tougher than them and Uno's and Duo's teams send them packing. The birds are smarter than the fish."

"Quatro and Cinco are leading the flights attacking the Killer Whales. Once again, we are too fast and agile, and we can fly so they are just killing themselves. Yikes! What a blood bath! Earnest is leading the flight attacking the Leopard seals. Our guys are so fast the seals wind up biting each other. Again, what a blood bath! The seals are eating each other. Before we can get to them, the other potential water dangers leave. Looks like they snacked a bit on the carcasses of the Leopard Seals and the Killer Whales before leaving. If we could have talked to them, we would have just told all of them to leave. We take no pleasure in their deaths."

"So, our enemies have been routed and are leaving the waters and the skies and it is safe to go in and have breakfast now. We have learned to feed another way and so we will stay here. You may have noticed that we are shape shifters now, yes? On the Star Planet every one of us is either 3, or 4 or 5 feet tall. We also have sort of archangel wings that are twice our height. We did not display that aspect of ourselves until it was necessary to protect the colony. But you can see that there have been enormous changes in us in what seems like the few hours that we have been gone. That is because we are time travelers also. Yeah, the future is bright for us! We were put to the test, and we ascended into the 5DC while we were away also."

"Anyhow, enjoy breakfast! We will be here when you get back. And stay away from the blood-stained waters you could get hurt. Stay in the open areas and you will have a peaceful breakfast. Uno you all go clean up in the Sphere first. Duo's team you go after Uno's team comes back. Then Earnest's team and then Quatro's team and then Cinco's team. Let's also keep an eye on the Colony and be careful the birds do not sneak back to attack our nests and young birds. I do not want a single loss today. Not a single loss!"

"Ruby, Ruby, Ruby! Dang girl, who would ever have thought of you as an Admiral or General. You did not miss a beat. That had to be the worst beating ever delivered by a band of Penguins. It humbles us to see how natural you are to all of this. We were going to make some suggestions, but we saw how good you were doing, and we just kept our mouths shut."

"Well, we could not have done it without all your help Boss, and I know I can speak for the whole Colony when I say that we were tired of losing. And I am underselling the tired! But we are off now eating fish, crustaceans, and cephalopods. So, on this planet, we are not really any better than the enemies we have just routed. I cannot live here anymore."

"I love my Colony, but I do not know who we are now. Who will we be on your planet? What will we do to define ourselves? Are we of sufficient character and skill and talent to be loved there? Looking at us here on our home planet I am not just really impressed. It is such a brutish existence. Kill to eat and be killed for food. Day after day after day. Wow!"

"Well Ruby those are some pretty darn deep thoughts for a Penguin. Look at how far you have come in the short time we have known each other. You are going to amaze yourself! You and your Colony will amaze each other, and you will be proud of each other and will never want to leave the paradise that is our planet. Except when you get to go with me, yes?"

"Well, you have that right, Boss! It would be special if we could go exploring with you every once and awhile. But only if we could help in some way. Not if we might be in the way."

"We will see how it develops Ruby, but I think you have only just begun, and the sky is the limit. And there is no pressure. You do not have to do anything. Just be yourself!"

THE COLONY LEAVES

"Okay, lets everybody come on into the Sphere now and find your places. We have a few procedures to learn and so the sooner we get in our places the sooner we can get done, yes?"

"Eighty-Eight has counted one thousand four hundred seventeen of you. That would be the ninety-seven of you that came with us already and another one thousand three hundred twenty of you that have been organized into forty-four groups of thirty each. These groups are for training purposes only. When you are not in training of one sort or another then you are free to associate with each other in such ever manner as is normal for you. For training purposes, we have organized you by age and sex and various other factors such as interests etc... Each of the forty-four groups is well balanced and has two assigned supervisors."

"The group of ninety-seven will be training you. They have been through it before and are experts at it now. You will be going outside of this linear timeline to train. We will be going with you, we will just be doing other things as you train. It is not that we do not want to do the work with you. It is just important that you demonstrate the ability to do this work as a species ability. And we have all the faith in the world in your group of ninety-seven."

"Your group of ninety-seven were able to do this in just under two decades outside of linear time. But since you all have a colony mind, and they are experts you might get it done in under a decade. However, I would not focus on the internal time because the external time will be no more than a few hours, no matter how long you take internally. So please just start relaxing with some chants and deep breathing and your group of ninety-seven will give you additional instructions. And they will be moving among you to help in any way they might or just to enjoy being in your presence. So, feel free to ask them any questions you might have or share any emotions that you might be having with them. There are no bad or wrong questions or emotions."

We know that some of you are worried if your children will be able to withstand this training and the trip. And that is the going and coming and everything in between. Perhaps Eighty-Eight, should answer this question. The most concerned are mothers and she is a mother, and she can relate to you and your concerns. Take it away Eighty-Eight."

"Thank you very much Ninety-Nine. Let's give each other a big hand to start with. You are all breaking the script with such courage and power and velocity. It must stun you too, yes? We met with a large group of your children this morning before you awakened and arose. They had been searching for those of you that had gone to our planet. They had eavesdropped on us. Accordingly, they had their consciousness expanded and instantly understood our language and were also able to speak it in a telepathic sort of way. Just amazing! They knew we were gone, and they went looking for us and they looked for us for hours until Sweet Pea and her friend Pushup found us. Nicely done, kids! Give them a hand!"

"Nicely done, indeed! Anyhow, all of you kids that did that please stand up now. Great! And any other young ones that are not standing up right now please raise your hand. Great, no hands! What this shows us is that the children of your Colony did not fear this event they were afraid of missing out on it. They even secretly participated in the early stages of it. They did so because it was the only way they were able to participate. So, mentally, and emotionally they are raring to get in the game and they took steps to be in the game. It is my expectation that they will find the entire trip far easier than the older members of your Colony largely because of their youth. They have far less baggage so to speak, yes?"

"They will be in multiple separate groups segregated by age and sex, and they will be led by supervisors that are a pending parenting pair who will be totally committed to their wellbeing. We get chills just thinking of how deeply committed these pending parenting pairs are to the children's wellbeing. Please stand up if you would. Let's give them a hand. Thank you!"

"It also is not us against the Universe. We will be within the 5DC consciousness of our planet and every being upon our planet. Every one of them will assist us with this safest of trips. Are there any further questions on this matter currently? Okay, then. Let's move on to getting ourselves in the proper frame of mind to make the transit successfully. Back to you Ninety-Nine!"

"Thank you, Eighty-Eight! This would be a good time to go to our inner world for growth and training. We will start by going to sleep. When we awaken, we will be cloaked in our training seclusion. After we complete the training, we will arrive right back here, we will acknowledge the training and we will commence with traveling at the speed of thought instructions."

"Spectacular! You completed all that training in just over five years! The colony mind in you is amazing. Thank you! Spectacular! So, where are we? I had marked my place. Yes, here it is. We will be guided by something like what your Earth scientists call Quantum Entanglement. You might think of it as consciousness controlling multiple physical objects across extended space and time at the same time. I know it works but I cannot explain it better than that."

"Look at this 3D representation of our Universe. Notice the Green arrow. It is pointing to your Mother Earth. We are traveling to the Planet from which we come identified by the Blue Arrow. It is a location roughly equidistant from the center of the Universe and on the opposite side of the Universe. Notice how the Universe is moving in an orderly and disorderly manner. We will not be traveling through this physical Universe, but we will be influenced by it. And it is influential. We are not even a speck on this map. Ha-ha! Boy is it ever influential!!"

"We will be traveling outside of space and time. Outside of the physical Universe where there is form but no-substance. And even so, it is a great distance to travel in such a short time as we will be traveling, but we can travel through no-substance easily. Since we can travel through no-substance easily we can exceed the speed of light which is the fastest one can move in the Physical Universe. That is the best I can explain it just now."

"To travel at such profound speeds and distances we must first achieve Unity. And to achieve Unity we must first achieve, in order, Love, Peace, Harmony and Tranquility. Starting with Love. Love is woven into the fabric which holds the Universe together. So, our transit will only be as successful as our ability to Love not just each other, but the entire Universe. That is why we must Love each other as one. So, chant with me if you would. I am one. I am one. I am one. Notice how there are one thousand four hundred nineteen variations of that chant. You can hear each one of us in the chant. I am one. I am one. I am one.... I AM! AND WE ARE! ONE! I AM! AND WE ARE! LOVE! Oh My God, this is exquisite. I am just soaring and expanding out into the Universe all around me. And so, I need to be at Peace because I am just so intrusive, I am banging off the walls. I Love banging off the walls. I just Love the sensation of the physicality of Love. However, being at Peace is being entirely devoid of any conflict or disturbance at all. So, I will focus on the Love of being present to the wonder of all that is around me without disturbing it."

"That is the essence of Peace. It is the Love of being present to the wonder of all that is around me without disturbing it. However, I notice that I am still banging into the walls so to speak and that is because there is a rhythm to the Universe, and we need to mimic it. We cannot go in a straight line if the energy vectors in the Universe are rhythmic, and we also do not want to travel right down the center of the freeway so to speak. We can uniquely harmonize with the energy vectors and slipstream effortlessly beside them."

"Through all of this and more we achieve tranquility. It is as if we are truly motionless. There is no sense of motion, and we are just absorbing the deep wisdom available from our passage. WE ARE! AND I AM! LOVE! WE ARE! AND I AM! PEACE! WE ARE! AND I AM! HARMONY! WE ARE! AND I AM! TRANQUILITY! WE ARE! AND I AM! UNITY!"

"Okay, how does everybody feel? Yeah, you cannot speak yet, yes? Ha-ha! Take your time. It seemed like just a short conversation, but we covered quite a bit of turf. Ha-ha! Please drink some water. There is a bottle for each of you, and I would not try to walk or even stand up until after you have consumed a whole bottle. Pass them around."

"Okay, okay, okay! We are going to rest for a bit as you all begin to become more active. Please do not summon us until all of you are fully awake and standing and walking about. Earnest will help you all locate your sleeping places. Thanks!"

"Thank you, Boss and Miss Boss! Wow! Is everyone else as whooped as I am? Ha-ha! I have done this a few times now and I still get very tired. And I am so happy we get to rest for a bit. Looking around it appears to me that the nap is unanimous. So, let's go to our wonderful colony sleep room in the back. I think that as soon as half of us are up and about then they should get the rest of us up. Otherwise, I say let the others sleep. Everybody in? Okay, then it is a deal. Adios!"

"I am 100% with you Earnest. Wait up for your Ruby, Luv!"

THE COLONY ARRIVES

"Wake up Ruby and Earnest, wake up! It is us, Sweet Pea and Pushup! More than ninety percent of the colony is up now, and we let you all sleep in because you seemed so tired when you went to bed, but we need you to get up now."

"Okay, Ruby and I appreciate your consideration for us Sweet Pea and Pushup! We were very tired. It has all been beyond exciting and that really wore us down. So, thanks! What's up?"

"Ninety-Nine and Eighty-Eight are getting everyone organized out on the extended outer deck of the Sphere now and they are all lined up in an orderly fashion in their groups. They sent us in to get you two and the rest of the first group. All of you all got to sleep in. The colony is so proud of you all. Come on, take our hands and we will walk out with you."

"Okay, here they come. Let's have a rousing round of applause for Ruby and Earnest! YES! Eighty-Eight and I just adore them, and we are proud of them beyond all measure. Absent your Earnest engaging in activities that he now regrets we would likely not have noticed you all. But we saw a picture of them with him comforting her and it touched us. And we came to meet them and introduce ourselves to them. And it quickly became obvious to us that they were soul mates, and that the young one was Earnest. It was not just the happiest of contacts in the first instance that they each realized that the soul attached to the young male's body was Earnest, but they have bonded wonderfully ever since."

"Since we came to make their acquaintance. You all are now on a 4DC/5DC planet on the other side of the Universe from your home planet with friends in high places, yes? So, let there not be a single negative comment on the matter. We have put it in our "things we have to do to entertain you file." We suggest you do the same. You may find it to be very helpful. Life can be hard to understand. However, every aspect to it seems to us to have some sort of entertainment value. We mean it would if we were watching a movie and saw it, yes? You have demonstrated the unique characteristics to be able to engage in and complete successfully every test to which you will be put to earn your conscious immortality.

However, that does not mean that you have not made errors in your life for which you feel remorse. Being able to express remorse and regret lesser behavior's is a required unique characteristic."

Let's extend our rousing round of applause to the first Ninety-Seven, now upon their second trip to this planet. Alright! We turn it over to the Ninety- Seven. They will be expanding your consciousness in what they feel is a warmer fuzzier introduction than they had. Ha-ha!!!"

"Thanks Boss! You are the best! Thank you for your kind introduction of me. I still feel a little sorrowful about my thoughts, actions, and deeds on that point, but I am glad you mentioned your entertainment file. Ha-ha! Ruby wanted to do me in, but she could just not keep from laughing when I used your quote. Nicely done, Boss!!!"

"My Beautiful, Beloved, and Blessed Colony! There is no need for you to follow exactly in our steps because we are here now and when we first came to the planet, we were the first ones and there were no warm fuzzies. Ha-ha! However, let us show you a few things that we have mastered in the interim. It is our belief that if we go straight to the mastering it will be better for such a large group as ours. I will throw a little powder on the apparent air in the open space leading to outside our craft. As you can see there is an invisible membrane between here and out there. This membrane shields us from the outside environment. We are 11 miles above the membrane separating the 4DC/5DC aspects of the planet. It is required for different atmospheres. As conscious immortals we can pass straight through either of these membranes without disturbing either of the adjacent atmospheres. We all are going to practice up here first. We the Ninety-Seven will demonstrate it can be done before we have you try. Think of the Big Bang. This is what the creator of the Universe did. Whatever you think out there you will create. So, if you think you will die you will. And if we think you will not die you will not die. And it is up to the most intentional and persistent thought, yes?"

"We will say it is best to skip the negative stuff and go straight to the amazing and miraculous and stupendous and the like. I know we are Penguins but let's think big out there. Watch now!"

"Oh My God, Sweet Pea! One-by-one, they each jumped through the membrane and then became a perfect ball of pure white light. Now they are making movements like a roller coaster with 97 cars. They are roaring down from above and make sharp turns up and down and left and right and you can virtually hear the Human Being children riding within the cars squealing in delight."

"Yes, Pushup! And now they are shapeshifting into what would have to be the coolest Penguin in the Universe. He is and then she is 97 feet tall and just perfect in every way. Moving faster than the speed of light they change positions and are in 97 different places seemingly at once. It is intoxicating to watch."

"Pure Penguin magic, my Luvs! Ninety-Nine and I are just amazed. Creative thought that only a Colony of Penguins could make. It could be a Colony of 97 or one of 1,417. Being both one organism and separate parts in the 5DC. Ha-ha! Not bad for newbies, yes? Let's give a big round of applause for the Ninety-Seven!"

"You all come back in now and we will get this trip organized to the 4DC below. Our people will be waiting down there. They have watched what you just created, and THEY LOVE YOU!!"

"Let's get everyone tethered and away we will go. I will go first, and Eighty-Eight will go last. And we are going to weave our way down there like skiers on an Olympic Mountain. Nothing fancy, just beauty, and class, and style, and joy and gratitude! One line more than a mile long hypnotizing those that watch us. Each of us in Love with the unified motion. We can do this, Luvs! We were born for this! This is our time to shine and shine we must! The entire Universe is drawing our greatness from us and reveling in it with us!"

"A Colony of 1,417 Penguins skiing the imaginary slopes of the 5DC in their first introduction to the 5DC and their humble servants weeping at the joy of bringing them here! Let's put some glowing headgear on so they can see us easily. Eleven miles straight down and thirty-three miles of movement crossing and descending the imaginary mountain. The joy, the endurance, the strength, the skill, the gratitude!"

PENGUINS ON THEIR OWN

"Nice work with the Penguins, Boss and Miss Boss! Ha-ha! They are natural comedians and laughter is always welcome. They have kept a distinctive Penguin motif, and not. Ha-ha! They have grown much taller and thinner, and some dress like 1920's movie stars. Ha-ha! They are so dramatic, yes? Ha-ha! But more of them dress like 1960's Beatnik's. So, we call them Beak Nik's. They are naturally very hip and cool and organic, yes? And they love poetry and literature and music and performing in both large and small venues. They have long legs and arms and hands now to help them with their performing. And they have kept the beaks and the sleek feathers, which they will dye, to retain their inner Penguin, yes? And their cranial capacity has at least quintupled. Anyhow, you Bosses are needed back on the other side of the Universe. You do need to return the Sphere to its rightful owner. So, what are your plans anyhow?"

"Thanks for keeping me on point Seventy-Seven! Did you all get the Penguins to clean it out yet? You know they can be an unruly bunch when they get to playing."

"Not in our job description, Boss. However, your Eighty-Eight made sure they cleaned the Sphere spic and span as you like to say. They are beside themselves with love for you two. I think they have left two beautiful Penguin stuffed animals with you for safe keeping. I would not be surprised if they named them Earnest and Ruby. You should keep them with you."

"Yeah, Boss! Because we might just pop into those forms and party with you while you are gone. We have brought some other things that might help you on your Gig!"

"Master Love, please call me Nines. My friends call me Nines. And having beheld the things I have to do to entertain you maybe you might want to call me Master Nines, yes? Ha-ha!!!"

"We have only just begun Master Nines - only just begun! We went into the Sphere and left these T-Shirts for you to take back to our Mother Earth, I thought of it, but Ruby designed them. The T-Shirts are every color of the canyon. They say "Ascension" on the front in large white or black letters. And they say, "So Easy a Penguin can do it!" on the back. Nice, yes?"

"Oh My God, you two are filled with the Love! It is just overflowing and bubbling out of you. Have you ever been this happy before? Have you even come close to this happy before?"

"No Master Nines, and what do we call Miss Boss? I mean, you often call her your better half but that seems more like a flirtation with her which we should not use."

"Well Master Love, we call Ruby Lady Master Light, and we call me Master Nines so we better have Master in there somewhere or it would not honor who she is. What do you think?"

"Yes, of course! We must have Lady Master in there because she is that for sure. I mean she is way above us and yet she treats us with much the same love and respect with which she treats you. I would like to give her a unique name that honors her uniqueness also. Yet, I keep coming back to Lady Master Nines which seems less unique. What do you think Lady Master Light?"

"I would say you might be overthinking it Master Love! I would say these two are one and he is the masculine principle, and she is the feminine principle, and they are the Nines, yes? Ha-ha!

I would say she is Lady Master Nines! And since Master Nines calls her his better half I would say if we would need something more unique then we should change his name!"

"Okay, Okay, you guys are natural comedians! Ha-ha!! Nicely done!! But since she is my Eighty-Eight then I think we may only rightly refer to her as Lady Master Eights!! Ha-ha!!"

"Lady Master Light, would you tell me who it is that is circling us as small Spheres of light just now? Is this another present for us or what?"

"Well, we may have some stowaways Boss! It is possible that it is Sweet Pea and Pushup. They told their folks they would just die if they did not go, and their folks did not want to test them."

"Do tell! Do tell! That is dangerous language to use on a 4DC/5DC planet, luvs. Planets such as this are very responsive to your thoughts, actions, and deeds and they can be very literal. You need to correct that right now! We will not go any further in the conversation until it is corrected. What do you say to remove this vile thought from our collective consciousness?"

"We are going to apologize to our folks for saying that. We will say it was never true, and we would never do that. And we will be filled with joy no matter what their decision."

"Nice, Sweet Pea! Have them communicate directly with us regarding their decision then. And based upon what they say to us we will decide if you can go with us or not."

"Okay, we just talked with your folks, and it looks like you are going to accompany us. They are excited for and proud of you both as are your friends and really the whole colony. You are the power and the creativity of those with an entire life ahead of them and you will see that the voices of such human beings are heard. You are immortal on this planet, but they are not so on their Mother Earth. Perhaps you can walk around in the form of Human Beings wearing your T-shirts? Or perhaps you can talk to these youth in their dream lands and help them to win their lives back! Anyhow, you all can go so you can materialize now! Ha-ha! And we will need to bestow Master names upon both of you also. But you must follow our lead as we progress! Agreed?"

"Yeah, Boss! We will be following your lead. I mean you are leading us back to our Mother Earth and we are going with you, yes? That's what you mean right?"

"Not exactly, but good enough for now. And you do remember that I can travel back through time and reverse my decision, right? And while I may seem like a nice guy, I can be stern!"

"Please, Boss! Quit! We are rolling on the floor laughing! You do not like being stern with us so being stern with us when needed will likely fall to Lady Master Eights. And that will work! Yikes!"

"But anyway, we are just so filled with Love for you all and all of life right now we are bouncing off the walls. And we just Love this expression of the physicality of Love!"

"Really? How about if Lady Master Eights and I join you. We also Love this expression of the physicality of Love! It is even better in a padded cell where you can make the building shake."

"Boss, we need to go to the Peace now, yes? No, no, no! We need to unite our Love as a single voice first, yes? And then we go to Peace and Harmony and Tranquility and then Unity."

"Yep! We will have Master Love and Lady Master Light lead us in the Unified Love affirmation. Pushup, you will be Master Peace and you will lead us in the Unified Peace affirmation. Sweet Pea, you will be Lady Master Harmony and you will lead us in the Unified Harmony affirmation."

"I will lead the Tranquility affirmation with Lady Master Eights leading the Unity affirmation. Whereupon we will then be rocketing across the Universe at the speed of thought."

"So, does anyone have reservations before we commence our transportation endeavor so to speak? Now would be the time to speak if there are any such thoughts or feelings! Anyone?"

"Okay, Lady Master Harmony and Master Peace have their hands up. Anyone else? Okay, Master Love has his hand up and up goes Lady Master Lights hand also. Who wants to go first?"

"I'm first! So, there is a body back on Mother Earth that looks identical to me, and it is alive. And if I go back there then it must die or not be born so to speak, yes?"

Are there any differences between us that I need to know about? I mean it looks identical to me and it acts like me and if someone asked me, I would say it was me."

"LMH, there is one major difference between you and the one who is now manifesting as your previous self. You are your immortal future self. You are the continuum of you. You both exist as you and similarly so does every other member of your colony so exist. They are also their own immortal future selves. They are the continuums of themselves."

So, if you go back to your Mother Earth, Lady Master Harmony, you will not look or act or think or feel like that version of yourself at all. But you will have immense love for that version. And you will be humbled by the contact. You will be humbled with this rare extension of consciousness into its future self with such velocity and clarity.

It is a blessed side effect of your seeking to be in service to your Mother Earth. Generally, it occurs over such long durations of time that it cannot even be perceived but as you have alluded to, you may have evolved a million years almost overnight."

"WOW! You were going to tell me that without my asking, right? I mean that completely alters my desire to go on this trip with you. Count me out! I Love it here. I was going out of gratitude."

"Yeah, it is against the rules to interfere unduly with someone's life path and so it is advisable to be answering a question when you divulge such information. Nice question, yes? Nicely done!"

"Okay, that appears to answer Lady Master Harmony's primary concern. Are there any others that still have questions or additional concerns which they would like to have addressed?"

"If we did go would it upset nature or something like that. Or would we be hunted by Humans and eaten or be domesticated as farm hands or house companions?"

"Yeah, Master Peace I would not take your cues from Eighty-Eight and me. We are pretty much the same as you. We are our immortal future selves from back then. And there were few like us back then. Our 4DC selves studied thoroughly and contacted much higher order beings and more and because of those efforts they knew we existed with sufficient leverage and intentionality that they created us. So, we came out of their consciousness, and yet we overlapped them. And we were able to do that because at this level of consciousness we are our infinite and immortal selves."

"We are now quite distinctly our Soul Body and not our Physical Body. Our Soul Body is our core, and we manifest the other bodies at will almost like clothing. At the birth of our 5DC selves, you could see the locus of our beings in our Physical Body's move out of the Third Eye Chakra into the Spiritual Body and then on into the Soul Body never to return. Voila! Infinite and Immortal!"

"We lived that way for some time in the 4DC before we decided to go on to higher ground and we arrived at our Star Planet. But prior to leaving we were just not visible to anyone other than ourselves and we did not trust anyone else knowing for most of our lives then. So, I would not expect to be treated well by Human Beings of that day. Especially not if you started talking or singing. Oh My God!! I can only imagine the cray- cray!! Ha-ha!! Ultimately, they would attempt to exterminate you when you resisted their abuse."

"It would be an all-out effort on their part. Sort of a religious war on you all to eliminate an abomination of their version of the so-called God's law or something like that. I think that would take a lot of the joy out of it for you and you all are so well loved here and such a great contribution to this reality already why leave? Yes? Thank you, Master Peace!"

"Great question Master Peace! That is why we operate the way we operate. We know that everyone involved has something important to contribute or they would not be here. So, the kids have set the bar high for you two Master Love and Lady Master Light. Any questions or have those brilliant questions filled you to overflowing?"

"Well, they have filled us to overflowing Master Nines. So, we will not be going with you, but we do have questions. Who will be providing the leadership for the Colony while you are gone, we have never self-regulated at this level of consciousness? We have just followed whatever you and Lady Master Eights have suggested we should do and that has worked beyond our wildest dreams but what now, yes? Do we have an election? Do you just appoint someone? Do we have a Texas Cage Match? Ha-ha!"

"Since you asked Master Love, I am going to appoint you. And no funny stuff, right? You can do this. The hardest thing you will have to overcome is flattery and there will be some of that. But you can do it. And it means something to you because you had been eaten by a Leopard Seal less than a year prior to our coming to visit you all and that was not a coincidence, right? You came back for your Love, Master Love, but you came back for your Colony also. Something told you they would be needing you more than ever and that drove you. Nicely done! You have the command presence, you have the humility, you have the humor, and you have the wisdom. There is no way that anything can go wrong! Be well and be the joy!!!"

"Wow! We have covered a lot of turf, but I am sensing that Lady Master Light has a question or two also, yes?"

"Yes, I do Master Nines. I want you to leave the Sphere here with us. It will ground us on the planet. It will help us feel safe and it will continually remind us, and everyone else, who we are. We still need some time to adjust. And without you and Lady Master Eights we may sort of shrink. This may have been millions of years of evolution for us in a very short time and it is far from over. I am getting younger, and others are getting older and at this rate we will all eventually be contemporary. It is so much to adjust too."

"Oh my! That is a reach! I would like too but I have several other important uses for it right now. But I could clone a version of it for you that would provide shelter and comfort, but it would not fly. Would that work?"

"We can stay in touch. We will establish the connection when we get back to Mother Earth. She is so proud of you for moving to higher ground. Her Heart Soars!!! It is hard to imagine for her that you all went ahead of her, but she wants you to join her when she moves up."

"Before we go, we would like to sing you all a few more songs. We will leave tens of thousands of songs in the Clone Sphere for you. They are recorded and you can play them on the big screen. It will be like going to the Earth movies or something. Yes, we have left movies also and histories and pretty much a library of the life and times of our Mother Earth and her offspring. It is all labeled in cabinets and drawers and what not. It will be easy to find. You will oversee all that media Lady Master Light. Lots of learning also. Some of it never seen on the Earth."

"Are there any more questions? From anyone? You are not limited to only one question. Don't get them started, right Master Love! Ha-ha!"

"You got that right, Master Nines, enough said on that point. So, what is next? It feels like you all are just about to leave. How are you going to say goodbye to everyone? We will all be so sad."

"Well, we are going to sing our way back to Mother Earth. We have picked a song or two to say goodbye to you all and when we are done with it, we will drop our mikes and disappear. So, get everybody in the Sphere now seated in the outer Sphere. We will use the inner Sphere as a stage. That way every one of you wonderful Penguins will get direct contact with us singing goodbye."

"Looks like everybody is here. Okay, my luvs! Please settle down. This has been the time of our lives. Being with you all on this great adventure. It is hard to imagine topping it. It has been just Wonderful! We will be leaving now. It is our duty to leave, and it is what is best for you all. You need to spread you wings now and design your own life on this marvelous planet."

"It has been our great honor to bring you here and to watch you evolve millions of years in such a short time. We are in awe of your courage and your competence. We are leaving a Sphere structure with all its archives for you. Lady Master Light will be the Master curator of the archives of the Sphere. All access is to go through her. Her word is final."

And you all will need a leader to lead and guide you and to birth you into a fully functioning 5DC organism. And for starters that leader will be Master Love. And you will decide on others later.

And you will need help in maintaining a state of joy at first and Master Peace will be there to help all of you when you seem to lose the joy. He has almost open access to joy! Really! Ha-ha!

And Lady Master Harmony will oversee innovation for the time being. She is irrepressible creative. But she cannot do it alone. None of them can. You are a 5DC being now. Act like it!

Have fun! This is as close to heaven as there actually is so enjoy yourselves. This is the greatest gift you could possibly have been given. Enjoy it! Anyhow, Lady Master Eights and I would like to sing two Love songs to you before we leave. There are millions of ways to express Love and Love it is just so vital to immortality.

The first song is about a higher order love. You will like it very much. It is a beautiful love song about higher dimensional love, yes? And it is an individual love song, but it might also be sung to a colony, yes? Ha-ha! You ready Lady Master Eights?"

"Yes, I am! The second song is beyond compare, but it is an important message for you so I will give it a shot. It is a song about self-love.

"We are leaving with so many memories don't you dare forget us. Ha-ha! Unless you do! Ha-ha! Do what you must do Luv's. Be the best you can be, yes? Display your self-love, yes? It has been a rare honor for us to accompany you upon your ascension. I don't want to go. Lady Master Eights is making me go. If I had my druthers, I would stay with you all forever."

"Yes, I am making him go. He is such a baby! He acts like a tough guy but he does not really like 3DC/4DC so we will probably be back in a just a bit. Hà-ha! Take care of my children! Boom!"

With that they are gone! And I look at Lady Master Light and she looks at me and she says "Alright everybody let's take a nap. This has straight up worn me out. Anybody else? Ha-ha! Thanks Luv's! They are having a gala in 4DC for us tonight and I for one want to look my best!"

"Oops! We are back. Ha-ha! Master Nines wanted to see if Master Peace and Lady Master Harmony might help some friends of ours. The little children on Mother Earth need so much help and Master Nines knows that they will just love you. So perhaps you two could sing some original songs for them. Additionally, our people down on the 4DC have made a club for you all in the main square below. They call it Sweet Pea & Pushup's Place. You might want to rock it tonight!"

"It would be our hope that you use it to sing and dance and teach others to do the same and it would be wonderful if you would compose and sing and play original songs there. The younger beings on this planet will love your style and your contact with the young ones on your Mother Earth. Perhaps they will send new songs for you also, yes? As will we from Mother Earth!"

"You two will be very well loved by the children on your Mother Earth so send them joy and gratitude and love every day and help them out. Be their friends in high places when they get into trouble. Because this generation of Human Beings is the one that will lift your Mother Earth into 5DC. This generation! Your generation! This generation, emitting Love, Peace, Harmony, Tranquility and Unity! This generation, filled with Joy and Gratitude! This generation, with you former Penguins helping show them the way! Bye! Boom!"

SO HARD TO LEAVE

"So Boss, are you and Miss Boss in here still? Yeah, Earnest and I thought so. It was a heck of a celebration that your 4DC peeps held for us last night. Just wonderful! They had created fish! They had created our favorite food from before we became awake and aware. These little fish made entirely from consciousness. Ha-ha! We laughed until we cried! Oh My God, there were also volunteers for each of us that formed a quantum bond with us. So, now we are each sort of tethered to this planet no matter where we go in the Universe."

"Anyhow they were so generous to us. We are just so humbled by their Love for us. These are genuinely magnificent beings. Words cannot express it fully. But it is in there at depth. Then we were mesmerized by Sweet Pea and Pushup after dinner. They picked a couple of songs that you would have loved and sang them in honor to you and Miss Boss."

"First came Sweet Pea. She got an acoustic guitar and a stool, and she sang a song right up our alley, yes? It was a song about a simpler time when there was music in the air and great changes were a foot. Though not as great as the current changes a foot. Ha-ha! Then she went on to another song that would have been loved by you. It was a song about immortality, and it was just so beautiful and on point Boss!"

"So much so that Pushup left his piano and got a guitar and joined her and they sang it again but this time as a duo. Which, of course, led to another song lamenting this sleepwalking species of human beings. Wow Boss, they picked these themselves! Boss, there was a packed house crowd and they just roared. What wonderful songs and Sweet Pea and Pushup performed them magically. Sweet Pea then left the stage to Pushup. Pushup was mauling his piano all night just dragging every possible note out of it. And then he sang a song about not wanting to go. People were laughing and crying at the end it touched them so deeply that he did not want to go."

"So why did you have all of us do all this performing anyhow Boss? I mean it was great! Do not get me wrong about that. But none of this is how we are on our Mother Earth."

"That is true, Ruby. That is true. But songs add so much more power and durability to emotional relationships. They are such an anchor. They love you but they will never forget the songs. There are people walking around the square down there right now singing those songs or such versions of them as they remember. I wanted them to remember you richly. If you left."

"It is not uncommon for Earth Human Beings to lose their memory later in life. There is a disease named Alzheimer's that will take it all from them. And the last thing they lose is the songs. It is hysterical. They might not even know their name or who they are, but they will know their favorite song from when they were 20. So, you just sing with them, yes? Yes!"

"Songs in concert like this allow for the entire species to revel in the event and they will now be able to sing these songs to each other and to you the next time they see you. Count on it. We took you as ambassadors for your planet and all its species. So, we granted you Human Being skills and talents so that they could get a feel for your Human Beings also. You did an exemplary job. Just a wonderful job. They know that your Human Beings come with a bit more baggage but they like you and the music so they will give it a bit of a go."

"We also brought you all because you are a Colony. You already have a sort of 5DC consciousness because of that. You have a Colony Mind and an Individual Mind. You are not a single organism on your Mother Earth, but you are much closer to it than your Human Beings are. You will easily flourish on this planet whereas they might not."

"So, you are here for many reasons. First, Love and Light, yes? Second, the Colony Mind. Third, your tremendous performing abilities. And, Oh yeah, for your humor! Ha-ha! Oh yes!"

"Well, Earnest and I talked after we got back last night, and we decided to go back. And then we talked to Sweet Pea and Pushup, and they decided to go back and on and on it went. Until now, we are all going back. It seems there is unfinished business, and that business is with you, yes? We are not leaving your side feeling that way, so you are stuck with us."

"Previously, we had thought that the Human Beings upon our Mother Earth were just like you just not as smart or kind or something like that. But we were mistaken. We did a little research last night after we got back from the Gala, and we found precious little evidence that there are many, if any, Human Beings from 5DC and above on Our Mother Earth. Furthermore, we believe ourselves to be the first 5DC Penguins in the Universe though our research on that position is in its infancy and you might say we are not unbiased in the matter."

"We are not sure what the future holds for us on Our Mother Earth, but we want to be in service and of service in the larger game and we will be. We will assist in the lift, yes? Yes! So how do we roll this back a bit so that we are on Our Mother Earth, and we are working on ascending with the planet into the 5DC and yet we are still just doing our Penguin thing?"

"Ruby, Ruby, Ruby! As always, you are in time and on time. That was exactly the conversation for you to manifest last night. Nicely Done! You are the Brilliant Light of your Colony! Now you have 100% participation in this, yes? It is not necessary that it be 100% but it is a joy that it is. We just love the way you all think as a Colony. Just Beautiful!! Very 5DC!"

"Instead of taking you directly back to your Mother Earth we will first take you to the heart of the matter. Everything will then make sense and you will see your Beauty through our eyes."

"Thanks for calling me, Boss, Earnest! That touched me coming from you and your lovely Ruby. But where we are headed now it would be best to address me as Master Nines and Eighty-Eight as Lady Master Eights. We will address you as Master Love, Ruby as Lady Master Light, Pushup as Master Peace and Sweet Pea as Lady Master Harmony."

"I see that everybody is good with that. Thanks so much! Where we are headed now is into inner space and out onto The Ceremonial Fields ("The Fields") of All Possibility and Potentiality. The stage upon which we will perform is so huge that we will each feel like we are each all alone. Every bit of training you have had with us has been focused upon this very moment. It will not feel like a stage at all but those to whom we will make our case consider it such. So, we have had you performing ever since we met you."

"You are perfectly prepared. You will rise to the occasion with power and velocity. You will rise to the occasion with honor and dignity and as manifesters of the TRUTH. You will rise as those who will not back down!"

"Even before you do that you will be rising as fresh as a Daisy. So, you all need to hit the hay and go straight to sleep. Really! This next leg is going to be challenging! As you all are so fond of saying, I am underselling the challenge, yes? Ha-ha!! So please pack it in and we will awaken you when it is your time and not a moment before."

"Will do, Master Nines! And we will be traveling in the Sphere, right? Because I am sticking to my statements about it grounding us. It is almost my world now."

"I understand completely Lady Master Light. That is not a trivial conversation. The Sphere is currently the most dependable and reliable of the many realities in which you are dwelling. So sleep with complete assurance that when you awake you will still be in this Sphere in the bed in which you have laid your body to rest, and your beloved Master Love will be right beside you."

THE FIELDS AND THOSE ABOVE

"Well Eighty-Eight, what do you think? Everything went just spectacularly! But did it change anything? Aside from this small crew of Penguins and their devoted 5DC fans! Ha-ha!"

"A good question. Another question is: Did it change everything? It appears that our planet has now adopted their Mother Earth. She announced it at the gala last night. No one there was prepared for that. WOW! She did not mention us or our Penguins in her announcement but what are the odds that her announcement is just coincidental?"

"I did not know that our 5DC planet could even speak to us. And we are used to interacting with her in a very rich psychic manner, but I have no memory of her speaking to us. Do not go there Ninety-Nine. I can hear all the jokes forming in your mind and I may have to whup you for some of them and you are driving this Sphere so do not, yes? Ha-ha!"

"It is the Penguins dear. I now find it hard to see much other than the many facets of humor in all that is around me. They really are natural comedians. You chose them well Love!"

"Just put this jalopy on auto pilot and come on over and give your Mama some sugar. The music has got me sort of stirred up and thinking about the joy of the physicality of Love, remember?"

"I am not putting the jalopy on auto pilot. But I admire the richness of your rebuttal to my thought humor. Thank God, I did not speak it aloud. Nicely played my Love! Nicely played!"

"Oh Ninety-Nine, you are so adorable when you get all proper and stuff like that. Are you sure I can't convince you to put the jalopy on auto pilot?"

"Okay, okay you know it is always on auto pilot. But the kids, dear. I do not know what it would do to them or to us for that matter if they walked in on us."

"I will lock the door then. We have been working in shifting fields of intergalactic consequence. We need some time off to recover and so do the kids. So, slow this jalopy down!"

"Okay I have rescheduled our arrival time at The Ceremonial Fields of All Possibility and Potentiality for a day later, Eighty-Eight. We can have that time to ourselves risk free, yes? Err Hopefully!!"

"Oh Baby, Oh Baby, Oh Baby!!! OoooLaLa!!"

"Sweet Pea is that you? Have you violated our privacy request? Sweet Pea? Make yourself visible and speak with us. That would be NOW Sweet Pea!"

"Okay, but what about Pushup? He is here too. And we would not have done it if we were not concerned. I mean we heard all this carrying on from Lady Master Eights, and we were worried. Then it got so quiet that we were even more worried. So, we came in through the walls and you were both sound asleep. We had seen you rest before but never actually sleep."

"So, we feared that you had died, and we got mirrors from that drawer over there and we put them under your noses to see if you could fog a mirror. To our surprise you could. Woo-hoo!! Are you getting the true joy that this is giving me Master Nines? I mean do I have to tell you how we had to cover your naked bodies or would you like Pushup to tell you?

"Ha-ha!!! Yes, Sweet Pea, I attracted this to me because this Sphere is a Higher Order being and it can take things quite literally, yes? I was the one and I owe apologies to everyone. But now out! You will speak to no one about this. Am I understood? Lady Master Eights and I are allowed our private time."

"Yeah, you are allowed it, but you seem to have trouble containing it. Ha-ha!! And it is too late to prohibit distribution we have already fully distributed it. But we will be leaving now so you all can get yourselves back together. Pushup. Do you think that is the smell of sex? I have heard it has a sort of smell. Yes?"

"That is above my current pay grade Sweet Pea. But I have my curiosities so to speak. I will let you know if I start becoming obsessed with them Sugar. Ha-ha!"

"Okay, okay I owe you one for that but very nicely played! Just very nicely played! We are going to speak with the big guns and all they will see in our aura is sex and related jokes. Okay, ixnay on that. We are rising out of just the most wonderful sleep that we have had since we started on this whole endeavor, and we slept so well because we joyfully embraced each other."

"Nice recovery Master Nines! Nice recovery! And we have quite a bit more time to sleep and so we are going back to hit the hay. Confident that we will rise with a smile upon our faces. But Sweet Pea asked me to ask one further question, okay? So, is the sweet phrase Oh Baby or Baby Oh?"

"Yeah, we were just leaving. Ha-ha!"

"Holy Cow, the stuff we must do to entertain them. I suppose you could say it could have been worse, yes? Let's start getting this gig organized."

"Okay! Everybody let's get up and get at it! All my sleepy Penguin brothers and sisters, my co-creators of miracles extraordinaire, my musical geniuses with unrivaled comedic bent, unass your bunks and let's meet our destiny! And I am not overselling it! It truly does not get any bigger than this! Ha-ha!!"

"Great! Let's all gather in the center of the inner Sphere and reenergize ourselves. First a period of gentle chanting to reconnect with all that is. And then a period to draw the energies from the farthest reaches of the Universe deep within us. Drawing it deep into every atom of our bodies and every aspect of our beings. Great, how is everyone feeling? Excellent, two thumbs up!"

"When we come into the currently active area of The Fields, we will be well above The Fields itself. The Higher Order beings will be pulled up tight upon it. They will resemble huge peaks and mountain ranges and we will have to spiral down to the stage so to speak. We will disembark and arrange ourselves as we have previously done. Then, we will sit upon the stage in an orderly manner until we are requested to speak. We will bath ourselves in tranquility as we sit just bathing in the wisdom all around us. It could be days or weeks, or months or years and we will not even move until we are requested to speak. This will not concern us. We are more than up to the task."

"We have been practicing for this passage since we first saw you as our beautiful Penguins. And under our parenting you have evolved millions of years as time has stood still. We have gained so much from this passage some of the Higher Order beings might be wondering why we have even come here. In fact, our presence may be irritating to them. So, we will chill!"

When I rise, you all will rise to stand with me. When I have completed my opening remarks then you will each move to your pre-appointed positions. If you get confused, then speak to her within your mind, ask your Lady Master Eights where you are to go, and she will direct you exactly to your position. Sweet Pea and Pushup will soar with their Cosmic Ascended Beak Nik Band into the center of The Fields but very high above it and the remainder of us will space ourselves equally around the outer extent of The Fields. But for now, be quiet and calm."

I AM THAT I AM

AS ARE MY BROTHERS AND SISTERS

SPEAK!

A SHORT INTRODUCTION

"Beautiful, Blessed and Beloved Ones. Thank you from the depths of our hearts for granting us this audience. There is perhaps little that we can say or think that you are not already aware of. Even so, we have come all this way into your sacred mountains and down onto The Ceremonial Fields of All Possibility and Potentiality to stand before you."

"We have come to you to ask for your allowance of our use of The Ceremonial Fields of All Possibility and Potentiality to thwart the use of thermonuclear weapons upon Our Mother Earth. We know that such weapons do not exterminate the souls of Human Beings but if they are unleashed upon our Mother Earth many Billions of Human Being souls may experience the truly horrible deaths of the 3DC and or 4DC vehicles that they have used to fully participate in these levels of consciousness."

"All the other destructions which such warfare will bring are truly better left unspoken. It likely cannot be overestimated by us and it could include the destruction of our entire Solar System and more. So, we are here to fight those bombs in the only way we can conceive of doing it without some expansive amount of extreme destruction and disaster."

We also come to ask your allowance of our use of The Ceremonial Fields of All Possibility and Potentiality to thwart other catastrophes attracted by the Human Beings upon Our Mother Earth. While those other catastrophes may produce worse damage than the bombs, they will not exterminate any Human souls. But again, the damages cannot be overestimated."

"In the 70 years from 1950 to 2020 the population of Human Beings upon Our Mother Earth grew conservatively from 2.5 billion to 7.5 billion. At that rate of growth, in 70 more years there will be 22.5 billion Human Beings or a nine-fold growth in only 140 years. That is just not sustainable."

"They had horrendous wars and pandemics when there were less than 2 billion of them. What will they do with more than a ten-fold increase in population? The prognosis for the near-term future of this planet is very grim.

This is a planet driven by sex, money, and power. The more people you have the greater the potential of the elite and others to exploit them in service to the accumulation of money and power. So, nothing will be done to slow the population growth. The monied and powerful people would have to puke up their money and power and that is not going to happen."

"The voracious consumption of Our Mother Earth from this explosive population growth suggests a species more like a parasite than a species of Human Beings. But this is a species of Human Beings simply careening from one obsession to another with no regard for the damage done. This species simply cannot achieve the maturity and character necessary in the time available to prevent cascading catastrophes and untold damages therefrom."

"We propose lifting Our Mother Earth into the 5DC to avoid these enormous pending catastrophes. We come before you with a small band of committed beings to do so."

LET ME STOP YOU THERE IF YOU WOULD!

"Indeed, Beautiful, Blessed and Beloved One. My apologies!"

BE AT PEACE, NINETY-NINE AND EIGHTY-EIGHT
AND BE AT PEACE YOU PARADE OF PRECIOUS
PENGUINS OR BEAK-NIKS IF YOU PREFER
HOW ABOUT A SONG?

"Yeah, we have sort of an outrage song that seems suitable. And we can sing it in the motif of an acapella concert choir. Okay, my Beak-Nik's, tune to this pitch and follow my lead!

And we sing our song and when complete I signal everyone to bow their heads and I turn and bow my head to the One that is the initiator of the Big-Bang and the Big-Suck.

"We can see what you mean about him being adorable when he gets all proper and stuff like that Eighty-Eight. And the betting on this side is that the sweet phrase is Oh Baby! Would that be correct Eighty-Eight?"

"Yes! Yes, it would Sir!"

"Perhaps "Top" would be a better address for me Eighty-Eight. It makes me more approachable. After all, I am all that is and ever was and ever will be. I am a singularity, there prior to the Big-Bang and after the Big-Suck and during everything in between. So, I deeply appreciate your song for me. It is one of my favorites. I love music! And I have always considered myself a champion of the common Human Being so to speak. So please refer to me as Top!"

"Will do, Top! Will do!"

"I am distressed by the tremendous destruction of everything that I am in your solar system. I am 4.5 billion years old in My Mother Earth. And my species of Human Beings is let's say 300 thousand years old and has only been writing for 50 thousand years or so. And yet we are right up on the edge by the thought's actions and deeds of My species of Human Beings on My Mother Earth. And even My Universe is at risk at this moment."

"While contemplating this course of events I am not entirely emotionally balanced. I am a bit peeved as you might say. Let us look at the years, 4,500,000,000 years to create My spectacularly beautiful Mother Earth and this species of Human Beings has brought it and potentially My Universe to the edge of oblivion in the next 4.5 years but certainly no more than the next 45 years."

"So Human Beings on the planet right now are destroying me, the resident in My Mother Earth at the rate of a billion years of planetary existence per each single current human year or perhaps it is only 100 million of such years per human year."

YOU ALL HAVE PERFORMED WONDERFULLY
BUT WE WOULD LIKE TO CUT TO THE CHASE
AND GET DIRECTLY TO THE POINT, YES? YES!

YOUR STAR PLANET HAS ALREADY ADOPTED
MY MOTHER EARTH PLANET
AND WE CALL HER FORTH FROM THE FIELDS
INTO THE TOP OF THIS CEREMONY

AND WE CALL FORTH MY MOTHER EARTH
INTO THE MIDDLE OF THIS CEREMONY
AND SURROUND HER IN THE IMPENATRABLE
UNIVERSAL DODECAHEDRON FORM
WITH TWO MODIFICATIONS

THERE IS AN ALLOWANCE FOR A
CONNECTION BETWEEN YOUR STAR AND
MY MOTHER EARTH PLANET AND TWELVE
ALLOWANCES FOR A CONNECTION
BETWEEN THE SIMILAR PLANETS
AND MY MOTHER EARTH PLANET

IN THE EVENT THAT MY MOTHER EARTH
IS DESTROYED THEN THE DODECAHEDRON

WILL CONTAIN THE DESTRUCTION
WITH THOSE BEINGS THAT HAVE ATTAINED
A FOURTH OR FIFTH DIMENSION OF
CONSCIOUSNESS ESCAPING
UP ONTO THE STAR PLANET

THOSE BEINGS STILL STUCK AT A
THIRD DIMENSION OF CONSCIOUSNESS
WILL ESCAPE DOWN
ONTO THE SIMILAR PLANET
TO WHICH THEY HAVE BEEN ASSIGNED
WITH OTHER SIMILAR HUMAN BEINGS
IT WILL BE A RIGOROUS TRAINING
THEY WILL GET WHAT THE GIVE

IN THE EVENT THAT MY MOTHER EARTH
IS NOT DESTROYED SHE WILL ASCEND TO
THE FIFTH DIMENSION OF CONSCIOUSNESS
ALONG WITH THOSE BEINGS THAT HAVE
ACHIEVED FOURTH AND FIFTH DIMENSIONAL
CONSCIOUSNESS AND THOSE BEINGS
STILL EVIDENCING A THIRD DIMENSIONAL
CONSCIOUSNESS WILL DESCEND
TO THE SIMILAR PLANET THEY ARE ASSIGNED

MY MOTHER EARTH HAS ALREADY ACHIEVED
FIFTH DIMENSIONAL CONSCIOUSNESS
BUT SHE HAS REQUESTED SOME MORE TIME
AND HER REQUEST HAS BEEN GRANTED
THANK YOU FOR YOUR ATTENTION
TO THIS MATTER
IT SPEAKS VERY HIGHLY OF YOU
THAT YOU CAME AND MADE THIS REQUEST
WE KNEW OF YOUR JOURNEY

AND HAD ALREADY GRANTED YOUR REQUEST

BUT HAVING YOU UPON THE FIELDS
WITH US TODAY IS A FIRST
THAT YOU HAD WORKED
SO HARD FOR
THAT WE DECIDED TO GRANT
YOUR PRESENCE HERE WITH US
KNOW THAT WE ARE WITH YOU
AND THIS IS A PRIORITY FOR US
LOVE AND LIGHT
BEAUTIFUL BLESSED
AND BELOVED ONES

TOP AND HIS TEAM
LIFE IS A TEAM SPORT, YES? YES!

"With that we are left completely in the dark vast emptiness of space. I think we and our Beak Nik's did just fine, Lady Master Eights. It went just like I thought it would. Ha-ha!!! Way over our heads! Ha-ha! I am so grateful and yet I am shaken to the core. I cannot believe how well you all sang that song my beloved Beak-Nik's. I was completely winging it, but you sounded like you had rehearsed it. Did you?"

"Of course, we did Boss! Pushup found it and loved it so much he taught all the rest of us. We played it in our little club. We just did not mention it because it seemed so sad. But I guess we were guided to it in some way. We are so glad we were! Top seemed moved by us singing it. So, what now Boss?"

"Well, Sweet Pea, I think this aspect of the fix went extremely well. The worst outcome is that Our Mother Earth gets destroyed but it is contained so nothing else in the Universe is destroyed and this species of Human Being continues in existence although some large number of them will find it uncomfortable for some time to come."

"So, that is our pound of cure, yes? The danger was so imminent that the pound of cure had to be initiated immediately and we have done so with the help of Top and his team."

"You did that all by yourselves my friends. You were my team in this initiative."

"Is that you Top?"

"Yes, it is Ninety-Nine. I neglected to mention that you all have received promotions so to speak in recognition of the nature of your conduct and character in this matter."

"The entire Parade of Precious Penguins are now Human Beings with no less than a 4DC level of consciousness. Quite a few of you are 5DC with Ruby, Earnest, Sweet Pea, Pushup, Aristotle, Nikola, Joan, Timothy, Paula, Priscilla, Penelope, Mack, and Dave and a few more not previously mentioned in that crew. It seems like Amadeus is hiding out in there also. And one of your prodigies is in trouble back on Our Mother Earth so the sooner you get back the better. A lover of Fairy Penguins if my information is correct, yes?"

"Yes, yes Top, the Angels are on site in my absence. But I have been very uncomfortable ever since I heard of the event."

BE AT PEACE
IT HAS BEEN BEAUTIFULLY HANDLED
WANTS YOU TO KNOW
EVERYTHING IS OKAY
WANTS TO APOLOGISE
FOR THE EVENT
THESE THINGS HAPPEN
SAY IT IS NO STEP FOR A STEPPER
SAY I TOLD YOU TO SAY THAT

I SAY INVITE TO TRAVELWITH
AND WORK WITH YOU ALL
WILL BE A GREAT ADDITION

"Ninety-Nine and Eighty-Eight, you have both jumped to the 6DC. You have exceeded all expectations. We are so grateful for your taking the initiative. And the best is yet to come, yes?"

"Yes, it is Top! The ounce of prevention is on its way. I have not recruited the team yet and I am glad you intervened before I did so that they would know the rewards of everything they have done so far. And their rewards are irreversible. They cannot be taken away. Which is perfect because that gives them complete freedom to participate or not. Thank you, Top!"

"You are welcome, Ninety-Nine!"

"Okay then, what is next? Ha-ha! You are going to love this. Hà-ha! I am headed back to Mother Earth with whomever will go with me. Back to the Mother Earth of as much as 300,000 years ago a bit before the predecessors of this species of Human Beings began emerging out of the animal kingdom."

"I or we are going to find those first ones and the next ones, and the next ones and I or we are going to establish structures around them, called reserves, in which they are completely protected not only from harm but also from the threat of harm. And we will interact with them and accelerate their growth and development over many lifetimes into a 5DC species of Human Beings."

We will do so perhaps as much as 100,000 years or more prior to the pound of cure and as such the pound of cure and all related matters will never happen. Our Mother Earth will be a spectacular planet. Other higher order beings in the Universe will have to wait long periods of time just to gain entrance for a visit there. Not because it is overpopulated but because it is carefully populated by a species of Human Beings that are stewards of the planet and all the wonderful life that flourishes upon her."

"Any questions? What's up Ruby?"

"Boss, are we going in the Sphere? If so, we are all in."

"Yes, we are going in the Sphere, Ruby. And you all need to get some rest in it right now and when you wake up you will be 9, 10 or 11 feet tall. You are 5DC Human Beings now, Loves! You can decide if you are coming with me when you are rested."

"Boss" "Yes, Ruby"

"Was this your plan all along? I mean it seems so logical in hindsight that it seems like you must have been planning it. Which, if so, that makes me a little uncomfortable. I mean what else are you planning that we do not know about?"

"Ha-ha, there you are again, Ruby! In time and on time. That does need to be addressed doesn't it. So let me address it. Because this is now going to be happening to you."

"In 5DC and above we exist in the NOW! We do not exist in between the past and the future. We make continual adjustments to the NOW as we are so moved and in so doing, we sort of moment-by-moment true up pasts and futures to be wholly and entirely consistent with our NOW because they are part of our NOW. And if we travel into the past or the future we continue to exist in the NOW with our locus in those points in space and time. We have dominion over space and time and so how could it be otherwise."

"Eighty-Eight and I did not come to your Mother Earth to do anything other than see who was moving in the 5DC over here and we still have not sought him out to meet him. Ha-ha! But we have his Sphere. We, quite unexpectedly, got locked into a war that we decided we could not bear to lose. We have initiated a massive pound of cure, and we are initiating a creative ounce of prevention that will be one of the great wonders of this Universe. It simply has not been done before in this Universe."

"In doing all of this we have enrolled you beautiful little loving beams of light, you in your Fairy Penguin forms, into the game. You accelerated way beyond what this species of Human Beings beginning 300,000 years ago will be able to tolerate. This next leg will be the easy part. Everything that was terrifying and hard and potentially harmful is behind you. This will be like an extended vacation in paradise. You will get to see your Mother Earth in her finest hour. You will see the waters cut the waterfalls into the mountains. You will see the great trees grow to enormous heights and thicknesses. You will see the magnificent array of colors she presents to the Universe."

"You will laugh endlessly about what sissies her species of Human Beings are even as you lovingly nurture them for several hundred thousand years in a manner that will alter the Universe. There certainly may have been some but we know of no Human Beings from the time in which we made your acquaintance that would have been able to do this. But we did not know this when we were drawn to you. We simply trusted our instincts and conducted ourselves in accordance with the nature of our higher order character. We stayed in the NOW and trusted our instincts."

"So, it will be for you. Because you all are a species of 4DC/5DC Human Beings now. But you will know of and will not forget your period in Penguin form and your transition therefrom and that will benefit the species of Human Beings upon this planet enormously. Because they came from non-human lineage also. So, you will be able to understand their fears and more easily comfort them."

"Mission will monitor you continuously. Our Mother Star Planet will be drawing your Mother Earth into higher dimensions of consciousness so that she no longer attracts lesser levels like those that have ravaged her and threatened the entire Universe."

"You will see the results of your work quickly as Human Beings with higher order proclivities begin dreaming about helping you and those that move into the 4DC/5DC arena begin showing up for duty at your door. That first knock will put a smile on your face, yes? Yes!"

"This will be a planet of peace in short order. You all will be at the center of it. Here are the keys to the Sphere. You all might want to sleep for quite a while to physically transform before you meet the first of this Human species that shows up."

"It will be an adolescent girl. She will show up right in front of your Sphere. You are to name her Joan. I do not think it will be difficult to find one of your own that will want to adopt her. So, the sooner you get to sleep the sooner you will get to meet her."

"We will not be hard to contact. We will be around and checking in. But you do not need any more supervision. Mission and Star will both be available to you at a moment's notice. We are headed back to our planet to make a pit stop and then on up into the 6DC. We are excited about that. But we will stay in touch."

Remember to stay in the NOW and trust your instincts and you will be extraordinarily well. How about a group hug for Eighty-Eight and me? It has been the greatest honor of our lives to participate in this with all of you. Thanks!"

"Wow, Ruby! I think they are really gone this time. What do you think?"

"Earnest, that straight up wore me out and we need to go get some rest. Ha-ha! Hey, wait for us you all! Perfect! Just Perfect! I bet we will sleep for six months. Come on baby!"

"Did you hear that? Was that a knock at the door? Oh My God, go get our Joan, Earnest. She appears to have a visitor throwing rocks at My Sphere. We may have to sleep in shifts. Perfect, I already love this place!"

"Okay, we are back. Please get everybody up and out into the large Sphere. And get Joan and her fellow foundation members in here in the small Sphere with Ruby and Earnest and us. Great! Eighty-Eight I think this is your moment, yes?"

"Yes, yes, it is, Ninety-Nine."

"Joan and Aristotle and Timothy and Nikola please come forward."

"So, Joan. Are you ready for this? Do you know what is about to happen? Have you prepared yourself emotionally for this?"

"Yeah, we thought not."

"Joan, there is an adolescent female whose skeleton will be found and immortalized as the oldest known member of the Human Species on the planet in the future and her name is to be Joan. And who will she say you are Joan?"

"You do not know because you have no idea how you will communicate with her. I mean she is almost a monkey of some sort. Right?"

"Well let's ask our language genius, Nikola. Nikola, what is the first word that you will teach our little one, our little Joan?"

"I will teach her the word Mother, Eighty-Eight. I will teach her the word Mother."

"And why will that be Nikola? Why will that be?"

"That will be because that will be the first word she teaches me with her language. And she will have a language. It will not be written but it will serve to communicate. And she will use it to ask me a question,"

"And what will that be?"

"She will take my hand and take me to Our Joan, and she will make her signs for mother, and she will take Our Joan's hand and smile at me. And I will shake my head yes and she will jump for joy and hop on Our Joan and hug and kiss her. And Our Joan will just cry and cry and cry for happiness!" "Like she and we are doing right now, Nikola?"

"Yes Eighty-Eight. Just like that."

"Are you going to be able to handle it my Love? We can have Nikola go with you to meet her for the first time. This is big, yes? You may even insert yourself directly into the genetic stream later, but you will be her mother Joan more than any later additions. You're mothering her will change all of it. So, get counsel every day. You have great helpers."

"And Pushup, Mack and Dave front and center. You three and Aristotle and Timothy are to always accompany Our Joan when she is outside the Sphere and No harm is to befall her. Right?"

"Absolutely Miss Boss!" "Thank you, guys!"

"Ruby, you will be Our Joan's mother figure. That will be quite a job so perhaps Nikola could be the Co-Curator of the Archives of the Sphere, yes?"

"Then you, Nikola, could do research on all the subtle movements that the New Joan and other newbies make that can be interpreted as language. And you can telepathically communicate with the ones outside to advise them of what you believe is being communicated. And you could also invent a unique language for them as well as tools and structures and such if that would be your desire. Does that interest you?"

"Absolutely, Miss Boss!"

"Great then! You all are perfect for this! Adieus Beloved Ones!"

"And, again, they are gone. They do not just stay around for a bunch of chit chat do they Earnest."

"No, they do not, Ruby. No, they do not."

"Uh guys, over here"

"What's up, Sweet Pea?"

"They may not be coming back this time, look! My sleep shirt has an Eighty-Eight on it and Pushup's has a Ninety-Nine on it. And they seem like they are glued to us. Ha-ha!"

Oh My God! That is fantastic! Do not be taking those off until they almost fall off. Quickly get a picture for the Archives Nikola!

Already done Ruby!

Wow! This is our gig now! We own it! Lock Stock and barrel! Open that door! Let's go for a morning flight. I feel like spreading my wings. Come on Earnest. Come on you raw bone Human Beings. Ha-ha! LET'S FLY!!!

www.ingramcontent.com/pod-product-compliance
Lightning Source LLC
LaVergne TN
LVHW050322190325
806018LV00001B/27